JUNIOR DRUG AWARENESS

Cocaine and Crack

JUNIOR DRUG AWARENESS

Alcohol

Amphetamines and
Other Stimulants

Cocaine and Crack

Diet Pills

Ecstasy and Other Club Drugs

Heroin

How to Say No to Drugs

Inhalants and Solvents

Marijuana

Nicotine

Over-the-Counter Drugs

Prozac and Other
Antidepressants

Steroids and Other
Performance-Enhancing
Drugs

Vicodin, OxyContin, and
Other Pain Relievers

JUNIOR DRUG AWARENESS

Cocaine and Crack

Krista West

CHELSEA HOUSE
PUBLISHERS
An imprint of Infobase Publishing

Junior Drug Awareness: Cocaine and Crack
Copyright © 2008 by Infobase Publishing

Chelsea House
An imprint of Infobase Publishing
132 West 31st Street
New York NY 10001

Library of Congress Cataloging-in-Publication Data

West, Krista.
  Cocaine and crack / Krista West.
      p. cm.—(Junior drug awareness)
  Includes bibliographical references and index.
  ISBN 978-0-7910-9704-5 (hardcover)
  1. Cocaine abuse—Juvenile literature. 2. Cocaine—Juvenile literature. 3. Crack (Drug)—Juvenile literature. I. Title. II. Series.

  HV5810.W46 2008
  613.8'4—dc22   2007024971

Text design by Erik Lindstrom
Cover design by Jooyoung An

Printed in the United States of America

Bang NMSG 10 9 8 7 6 5 4 3 2 1

This book is printed on acid-free paper.

CONTENTS

Battling a Pandemic: A History of Drugs in the United States

When Johnny came marching home again after the Civil War, he probably wasn't marching in a very straight line. This is because Johnny, like 400,000 of his fellow drug-addled soldiers, was addicted to morphine. With the advent of morphine and the invention of the hypodermic needle, drug addiction became a prominent problem during the nineteenth century. It was the first time such widespread drug dependence was documented in history.

Things didn't get much better in the later decades of the nineteenth century. Cocaine and opiates were used as over-the-counter "medicines." Of course, the most famous was Coca-Cola, which actually did contain cocaine in its early days.

After the turn of the twentieth century, drug abuse was spiraling out of control, and the United States government stepped in with the first regulatory controls. In 1906, the Pure Food and Drug Act became a law. It required the labeling of product ingredients. Next came the Harrison Narcotics Tax Act of 1914, which outlawed illegal importation or distribution of cocaine and opiates. During this time, neither the medical community nor the general population was aware of the principles of addiction.

After the passage of the Harrison Act, drug addiction was not a major issue in the United States until the 1960s, when drug abuse became a much bigger social problem. During this time, the federal government's drug enforcement agencies were found to be ineffective. Organizations often worked against one another, causing counterproductive effects. By 1973, things had gotten so bad that President Richard Nixon, by executive order, created the Drug Enforcement Administration (DEA), which became the lead agency in all federal narcotics investigations. It continues in that role to this day. The effectiveness of enforcement and the so-called "Drug War" are open to debate. Cocaine use has been reduced by 75% since its peak in 1985. However, its replacement might be methamphetamine (speed, crank, crystal), which is arguably more dangerous and is now plaguing the country. Also, illicit drugs tend to be cyclical, with various drugs, such as LSD, appearing, disappearing, and then reappearing again. It is probably closest to the truth to say that a war on drugs can never be won, just managed.

Fighting drugs involves a three-pronged battle. Enforcement is one prong. Education and prevention is the second. Treatment is the third.

Although pandemics of drug abuse have been with us for more than 150 years, education and prevention were not seriously considered until the 1970s. In 1982, former First Lady Betty Ford made drug treatment socially acceptable with the opening of the Betty Ford Center. This followed her own battle with addiction. Other treatment centers—including Hazelton, Fair Oaks, and Smithers (now called the Addiction Institute of New York)—added to the growing number of clinics, and soon detox facilities were in almost every city. The cost of a single day in one of these facilities is often more than $1,000, and the effectiveness of treatment centers is often debated. To this day, there is little regulation over who can practice counseling.

It soon became apparent that the most effective way to deal with the drug problem was prevention by education. By some estimates, the overall cost of drug abuse to society exceeds $250 billion per year; preventive education is certainly the most cost-effective way to deal with the problem. Drug education can save people from misery, pain, and ultimately even jail time or death. In the early 1980s, First Lady Nancy Reagan started the "Just Say No" program. Although many scoffed at the program, its promotion of total abstinence from drugs has been effective with many adolescents. In the late 1980s, drug education was not science based, and people essentially were throwing mud at the wall to see what would stick. Motivations of all types spawned hundreds, if not thousands, of drug-education programs. Promoters of some programs used whatever political clout they could muster to get on various government agencies' lists of most effective programs. The bottom line, however, is that prevention is very difficult to quantify. How do you prove that drug use would have occurred if it were not prevented from happening?

In 1983, the Los Angeles Unified School District, in conjunction with the Los Angeles Police Department, started what was considered at that time to be the gold standard of school-based drug education programs. The program was called Drug Abuse Resistance Education, otherwise known as D.A.R.E. The program called for specially trained police officers to deliver drug-education programs in schools. This was an era in which community-oriented policing was all the rage. The logic was that kids would give street credibility to a police officer who spoke to them about drugs. The popularity of the program was unprecedented. It spread all across the country and around the world. Ultimately, 80% of American school districts would utilize the program. Parents, police officers, and kids all loved it. Unexpectedly, a special bond was formed between the kids who took the program and the police officers who ran it. Even in adulthood, many kids remember the name of their D.A.R.E. officer.

By 1991, national drug use had been halved. In any other medical-oriented field, this figure would be astonishing. The number of people in the United States using drugs went from about 25 million in the early 1980s to 11 million in 1991. All three prongs of the battle against drugs vied for government dollars, with each prong claiming credit for the reduction in drug use. There is no doubt that each contributed to the decline in drug use, but most people agreed that preventing drug abuse before it started had proved to be the most effective strategy. The National Institute on Drug Abuse (NIDA), which was established in 1974, defines its mandate in this way: "NIDA's mission is to lead the Nation in bringing the power of science to bear on drug abuse and addiction." NIDA leaders were the experts in prevention and treatment, and they had enormous resources. In

1986, the nonprofit Partnership for a Drug-Free America was founded. The organization defined its mission as, "Putting to use all major media outlets, including TV, radio, print advertisements and the Internet, along with the pro bono work of the country's best advertising agencies." The Partnership for a Drug-Free America is responsible for the popular campaign that compared "your brain on drugs" to fried eggs.

The American drug problem was front-page news for years up until 1990–1991. Then the Gulf War took over the news, and drugs never again regained the headlines. Most likely, this lack of media coverage has led to some peaks and valleys in the number of people using drugs, but there has not been a return to anything near the high percentage of use recorded in 1985. According to the University of Michigan's 2006 Monitoring the Future study, which measured adolescent drug use, there were 840,000 fewer American kids using drugs in 2006 than in 2001. This represents a 23% reduction in drug use. With the exception of prescription drugs, drug use continues to decline.

In 2000, the Robert Wood Johnson Foundation recognized that the D.A.R.E. Program, with its tens of thousands of trained police officers, had the top state-of-the-art delivery system of drug education in the world. The foundation dedicated $15 million to develop a cutting-edge prevention curriculum to be delivered by D.A.R.E. The new D.A.R.E. program incorporates the latest in prevention and education, including high-tech, interactive, and decision-model-based approaches. D.A.R.E. officers are trained as "coaches" who support kids as they practice research-based refusal strategies in high-stakes peer-pressure environments. Through stunning magnetic resonance imaging (MRI) images, students get to see tangible proof of how various substances diminish brain activity.

Will this program be the solution to the drug problem in the United States? By itself, probably not. It is simply an integral part of a larger equation that everyone involved hopes will prevent kids from ever starting to use drugs. The equation also requires guidance in the home, without which no program can be effective.

Ronald J. Brogan
Regional Director
D.A.R.E America

1

Cocaine in Society

Many people are already somewhat familiar with cocaine and crack. They've read dramatic news stories about drug dealers, determined law enforcement agents, and wealthy and drug-addicted celebrities. Still, learning the basic history and science of cocaine and crack is the first step in understanding the importance, impact, and influence of this drug today.

Cocaine is a drug that is found naturally in the leaves of the South American coca plant. Crack (also known as crack cocaine) is a solid, rocklike form of cocaine. Both are highly addictive, illegal drugs often used for recreational purposes. And both are considered stimulants.

A **stimulant** is a drug that does two things: First, it stimulates, or increases, physical processes in the human body (such as the heart beat and breathing); and second, it makes a person feel intense emotions for a brief period of time. Together, these two effects have helped make cocaine and crack very popular and very problematic drugs.

POPULAR AND PROBLEMATIC

Cocaine is clearly popular. According to the 2005 National Survey on Drug Use and Health (NSDUH) from the federal Substance Abuse and Mental Health Services Administration (SAMHSA), almost 34 million Americans above age 12—about 14%—have tried cocaine at least once in their lives. This includes 3% of eighth graders, 5% of tenth graders, and 9% of twelfth graders, according to another ongoing research project called Monitoring the Future (MTF). MTF is a study funded by the National Institute on Drug Abuse and carried out by scientists at the University of Michigan Survey Research Center. Only marijuana, says both the NSDUH and MTF, is a more popular illegal drug in this country.

Cocaine is clearly problematic. On the national scale, the U.S. government spends billions of dollars each year to better understand and control illegal drug use. The White House Office of National Drug Control Policy's (ONDCP) Drug Policy Information Clearinghouse Fact Sheet says the country spent about $36 billion to fight cocaine in 2000, the most recent year for which statistics are available.

On the human scale, cocaine simply hurts people deeply. Exactly how many people are hurt or killed each year by cocaine is very difficult to determine. But cocaine is the most common drug reported in hospital emergency room visits nationwide, according to the

Some cocaine addicts use a tool with a straight edge to push the powdered drug into a line that can be more easily sniffed.

Drug Abuse Warning Network (DAWN). DAWN is a public health surveillance system that is operated by the U.S. Department of Health and Human Services. The network monitors drug-related emergency room visits and deaths. In 2005, reports DAWN in the ONDCP's *Drug Facts: Cocaine*, about 30% of that year's 1.5 million drug-related emergency room visits—nearly 500,000 cases—involved cocaine. That's almost as many people as the entire population of the state of Wyoming.

Many of the people affected by cocaine are well-known celebrities, athletes, and politicians. But many, many more are normal people who have regular occupations. People of all ages, shapes, sizes, and classes are vulnerable to the temptations of cocaine addiction. More often than some people realize, cocaine kills. But it is possible to find treatment and beat a cocaine addiction.

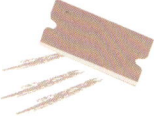

DRUGS AND THE U.S. GOVERNMENT

The more one reads about cocaine and other illegal drugs, the more likely one is to come across organizations that go by letter-heavy names such as NIDA, ONDCP, and DEA. Many of these are government agencies, each designed to understand or combat illegal drug abuse in the United States.

A government agency is an organization that is funded by taxpayer dollars and is intended to serve the country in some way: by providing information, collecting information, or regulating something. Because illegal drugs are a big and complicated issue in the United States, there are a lot of different drug agencies, each with its own role and mission. To help keep them straight, here is a rundown of some of the big federal drug agencies in this country.

AGENCY	ROLE
Drug Enforcement Agency (DEA) http://www.dea.gov	Enforces the laws and regulations of the United States and works to find people growing, dealing, and importing illegal drugs internationally. Part of the U.S. Department of Justice.
National Drug Intelligence Center (NDIC) http://www.usdoj.gov/ndic	Gathers information on drug dealing and abuse trends in the United States, and uses that information to help enforce the laws in this country. Part of the U.S. Department of Justice.

(continues on page 16)

(continued from page 15)

AGENCY	ROLE
National Institute on Drug Abuse (NIDA) http://www.nida.nih.gov	Supports scientific research on drug abuse and addiction. Part of the National Institutes of Health, Department of Health and Human Services.
Office of National Drug Control Policy (ONDCP) http://www.whitehouse drugpolicy.gov	Establishes policies, priorities, and objectives for the country's drug control program. Part of the Executive Office of the President.
Substance Abuse and Mental Health Services Administration (SAMHSA) http://www.samhsa.gov	Works to improve the lives of people with mental health and substance abuse problems. Part of the National Institutes of Health, Department of Health and Human Services.

Here is a rundown of famous people who have battled cocaine and lost—and a few who beat the odds.

COCAINE IN MUSIC

Bobby Hatfield was half of the 1960s singing duo the Righteous Brothers, famous for many songs, including "Unchained Melody" and "You've Lost That Loving Feeling." In 2003, hours before a concert in Kalamazoo, Michigan, several news sources reported that hotel staff found Hatfield dead in his hotel bed. A heart attack was ruled as the cause of death, but a later autopsy revealed cocaine as the ultimate cause of that heart attack. Hatfield had died of a cocaine overdose at 63 years old.

Shannon Hoon was the lead singer for the rock group Blind Melon, a popular band in the early 1990s perhaps best known for a music video that features a slightly overweight, dancing girl in a bumblebee costume. While awaiting an evening show in New Orleans, Hoon entered the band's tour bus and never

COCAINE FACTS AND FIGURES

Sometimes numbers speak louder than words. Statistics on cocaine use and abuse in the United States support the idea that cocaine is a popular and problematic illegal drug. The following cocaine facts and figures are from the Greater Dallas Council on Alcohol and Drug Abuse Web site.

- Cocaine is the second most common illegal drug (marijuana is number one).
- One in 10 workers knows someone who uses cocaine on the job.
- People age 18 to 25 currently have the highest rate of cocaine use.
- Up to 75% of people who try cocaine will become addicted to it.
- Only 25% of people who try cocaine will be able to quit without help.
- Every day, more than 5,000 people experiment with cocaine for the first time.

came out, according to accounts in *Rolling Stone* magazine and other sources. A friend found him dead inside the bus. Hoon had died of a cocaine and heroin overdose at the peak of his music career in 1995. He was 28 years old.

COCAINE ON SCREEN

Chris Farley was a comedian and actor remembered for his five years working on *Saturday Night Live* and for playing lovable slobs in movies. Many newspaper reports said Farley was seen drinking heavily in the days before his death, and that he fought drug and food addictions for years. Farley's brother found him dead on the floor of his own apartment building in 1997. He had died of a cocaine and morphine overdose. He was 33 years old.

Mary Anissa Jones was a child actress known as "Buffy" in the 1960s sitcom *A Family Affair*. After the popular sitcom ended she began shoplifting, using drugs, and skipping school. When she turned 18, Jones gained control of her television earnings and moved into an apartment with her brother. According to news reports in 1976, after partying at a friend's house one night she was found dead in a bed. Jones had died of a severe cocaine overdose at 18 years old.

River Phoenix was an Academy Award–nominated actor who starred in many movies, including *Stand by Me*, *Running on Empty*, and *My Own Private Idaho*. On Halloween night in 1993, Phoenix was partying with friends and his brother, actor Joaquin Phoenix, at a Hollywood nightclub and reportedly began having seizures. Friends called 911, but Phoenix stopped breathing and was unable to be revived. Many movie critics thought Phoenix had huge potential as an actor, but his career and life were cut short by an overdose of a mix

Actor River Phoenix starred in films alongside Harrison Ford, Sidney Poitier, Keanu Reeves, and Uma Thurman. His life was cut short when he overdosed on a potent mixture of drugs, including cocaine and heroin, on October 31, 1993.

of drugs that included cocaine and heroin. He was 23 years old.

COCAINE IN SPORTS

Len Bias was a college basketball star selected by the Boston Celtics in the NBA's second-round draft in 1986. He was often compared to star player Michael Jordan, and was widely believed to be one of the most dynamic young stars of the game. But less than 48 hours after the draft—and soon after passing numerous

COOLING DOWN ON COCAINE

Scientists have discovered that cocaine use prevents an overheated human body from cooling down, according to a study reported in *Scientific American*: "Cocaine Curtails the Body's Ability to Cool Off." When cocaine is used at hot, sweaty, nightclubs and parties, even a small amount of the drug disturbs the body's ability to lower its temperature—sometimes with fatal consequences.

Scientists have long known that cocaine use can increase a person's body temperature. But now they know it also increases sweating and prevents blood vessels on the skin from opening to release the body's extra heat. As a result, cocaine users simply don't realize they are getting hot. Without knowing they are hot, users are unlikely to drink water or find cooler temperatures.

Although this effect is not entirely understood, the study authors suggest that perhaps this is one reason why so many overdose deaths occur at nightclubs and parties where cocaine users often become overly hot and sweaty.

College basketball player Len Bias put on a Boston Celtics hat after being selected as the number two pick in the NBA draft on June 17, 1986. Two days later he died of a cocaine overdose in a Maryland dormitory room during a party to celebrate his success.

professional basketball drug tests—Bias collapsed in his dorm room. He had died of a cocaine overdose at 22 years old.

Marco Pantani was a professional cyclist from Italy who won the Tour de France in 1998 and was known for his ability to power up hills on his bike. Nicknamed "The Pirate," Pantani was disqualified from a bike race in 1999 for testing positive for performance-enhancing drugs, and as a result developed a bad reputation in the world of professional cycling. Five years later, in 2004, staff members in an Italian hotel found his dead body. Pantani had died of a cocaine overdose at 34 years old.

LIFE AFTER ADDICTION

Marion Barry served as the mayor of Washington, D.C., from 1979 to 1991 and from 1995 to 1999. Barry is often credited with balancing the city's budget, creating jobs, and reinvigorating the downtown area during his time in office. But in 1990, he was arrested for possession and use of crack cocaine and served six months in prison. When Barry got out of jail, he again ran for mayor and won his job back. Today he serves on the city council representing one of the poorest neighborhoods in Washington, D.C. In 2005, some news sources reported that Barry again tested positive for cocaine during a mandatory drug test. At about the same time, Barry was convicted for not paying taxes, and the tax trouble overshadowed the drug test results in the media. Today, Barry is in his 70s and continues his successful career as a politician.

Richard Pryor was a comedian and actor especially popular throughout the 1960s, 1970s, and 1980s, appearing in more than 40 movies, including *Superman III* and *The Toy*. In 1980, Pryor reportedly accidentally set himself on fire while freebasing, or smoking, cocaine. The event made public Pryor's long-time addiction to cocaine and alcohol. As early as 1960, Pryor was using $100 worth of cocaine per day. Cocaine addiction reportedly caused Pryor to have three non-fatal heart attacks during the years that followed. But somehow he didn't die from his addiction. Pryor, who suffered from multiple sclerosis (MS), a disease of the central nervous system, died in 2005 of a heart attack unrelated to cocaine. He was 65 years old.

Dennis Quaid is an actor who has starred in dozens of movies, including *Breaking Away*, *The Right Stuff*, and *The Parent Trap*. In the 1970s, Quaid became addicted to cocaine. In an interview on *Larry King Live* in 2002, Quaid said he had a near-death experience and decided to get help to quit cocaine. He had tried to quit before on his own, but without success. After spending time at a rehabilitation clinic and not working for two years, Quaid successfully stopped using cocaine in the late 1980s. He's now working steadily as an actor again.

2

The History of Cocaine

Tracing the history of cocaine is a three-step trek around the world. The story begins on the northwestern coast of South America, where cocaine has grown naturally and been used by native peoples for thousands of years. Next, foreign explorers conquer South American communities, and cocaine crosses the ocean to Europe. There the drug is legally used, studied, and sold. Soon cocaine becomes valuable both economically and socially. Finally, cocaine arrives in the United States. Eventually its widespread, illegal use and abuse prompts multiple education and law enforcement programs on the national scale.

Cocaine's story begins humbly, but erupts slowly over hundreds of years into the tale we know today: cocaine's powerful role in the past and the present.

COCAINE IN SOUTH AMERICA

Cocaine leaves grow on trees, and the earliest known use of cocaine dates back nearly 5,000 years, to sometime in the year 3000 B.C. At this point in history, no large civilizations were known to exist in northwestern South America where cocaine grows naturally, but many small tribes existed. Scientists studying the remains of these ancient peoples have found evidence that cocaine was ingested and used, perhaps quite commonly. In southwestern Ecuador and northern Chile, for example, scientists have unearthed graves more than 4,000 years old. Hairs from human mummies in these graves were found to contain traces of cocaine. This is because once a person ingests cocaine, parts of the drug are deposited in the hair and remain there long after death.

In what is now northern Peru, another country in South America, drawings on old pots and other artifacts show cocaine being chewed by humans. One 2,500-year-old pot made by the Moche tribe shows people with their cheeks full of cocaine leaves and carrying gourds full of the leaves.

Similar gravesites and images of cocaine use are depicted throughout the ancient cultures of South America. The drug was often used in religious ceremonies, including funerals. Eventually all of these small, cocaine-using tribes on the western coast of South America were taken over by the Inca Empire, sometime in the 1400s.

At its peak, the Inca Empire included about 12 million people and stretched 2,500 miles (4,000 kilometers) along the western coast of South America. The Inca were organized and successful, and they greatly expanded the area's agricultural crops, including cocaine crops. But the new Inca rulers widely regulated use of the popular coca leaves. The ruling Inca family appointed official

For thousands of years, coca plants have been growing naturally along South America's northwestern coast.

cocaine collectors, who gathered all the cocaine that was grown and turned it over to the royal family.

At this point in time, cocaine use apparently was reserved only for the royal Inca and special subjects or rituals. Priests, victims of human sacrifice, slave workers, and visitors were occasionally given cocaine. Experts suggest that the Inca were clearly aware of the physical powers and value of cocaine.

The Inca ruled much of South America until Spanish explorers arrived in the 1500s. Once the Spanish arrived, everything changed. According to accounts from early Spanish explorers visiting South America, the native people believed cocaine was a gift from the gods, or, more specifically, from one goddess.

The goddess figure that many natives credited with giving humans cocaine was known as "Mama Coca." Accounts of Mama Coca's gift vary with different legends, but in Steven B. Karch's book *A Brief History of Cocaine*, the Spanish explorer Viceroy Toledo describes the story this way:

> Among the natives there was a legend that before the coca tree was as it is now there was a beautiful woman, and because she lived a loose life they killed her and cut her body in two. From her body grew the bush that they call Mama-Coca, and from that time they began to eat it.

To the early Spanish explorers, cocaine was more of a cultural curiosity than a potentially valuable and unusual drug. They were just leaves off a tree, after all. At the time, the Spanish were much more interested in the natural deposits of gold and silver found on Inca land.

The Spanish eventually conquered the Inca and forced the native people to work in gold and silver mines. The Spanish then realized that when the native slaves chewed cocaine leaves, they were able to work long hours without rest or food. Cocaine began to look much more interesting to the Spanish, or at least worth further study.

A BRIEF HISTORY OF COCAINE

DATE	EVENT
3000 B.C.	Chewing coca leaves is widely practiced among native people in South America.
1400s	The Inca Empire takes control of coca crops in South America.
c. 1505	The first accounts of coca use make their way to Europe.
1550s	Peru helps mass produce and market coca.
1662	The poem "A Legend of Coca" is published by Abraham Cowley; marks the first time cocaine is mentioned in English literature.
1700s	Cocaine gains value as a medicine.
1835	Botanist Sir William Hooker publishes the first accurate drawing of the coca leaf in the *Companion to the Botanical Magazine*.
1855	Pure cocaine first extracted from the coca leaf.
1862	The Merck Company produces and sells about 1/4 pound of cocaine a year.
1870	Vin Mariani (wine containing coca) is sold widely in Europe.
1883	The Merck Company produces and sells about 3/4 pound of cocaine a year.

Cocaine was soon imported to Europe along with gold, silver, coffee, tea, and tobacco. But because it took so long for goods to cross the ocean by ship, the coca leaves lost their potency before reaching land in Europe. For a few hundred years, no one in Europe cared much

1884	Cocaine used as a numbing substance in eye surgery. Sigmund Freud publishes *On Coca*, recommending medicinal cocaine use.
1885	Parke-Davis begins to manufacture and sell pure cocaine powder in the United States.
1886	Coca-Cola, containing caffeine and cocaine, is introduced.
1901	Coca-Cola removes cocaine.
1905	Snorting cocaine powder becomes popular.
1910	First cases of nose damage from snorting cocaine are seen in hospitals and in medical literature.
1912	The United States reports 5,000 cocaine-related fatalities in one year.
1914	Cocaine becomes illegal in the United States.
1922	37 U.S. states prohibit depictions of drug use in the movies.
1961	The United States bans the production and trade of cocaine, opium, and marijuana.
1970s	Cocaine use peaks in the United States.
1980s	Crack, a cheaper form of cocaine, comes to the United States.
1992	The National Institute on Drug Abuse says 2 percent of all babies born in the United States are exposed to cocaine before birth.

for dried-up, de-drugged coca leaves. It took a while for Europeans to rediscover cocaine.

COCAINE IN EUROPE

It is difficult, if not impossible, to put an exact date on when Europeans first realized the value of cocaine. For hundreds of years, coca leaves were imported from South America but arrived dry and de-drugged. The leaves were so old that ingesting them no longer produced any special effects on the body.

Sometime in the mid- to late 1700s, British scientists studying plants began to take an interest in growing coca leaves. At first, they tried to grow coca leaves simply because they were exotic and unusual. But they soon realized that the cocaine-producing plants could be worth money and have a purpose.

By this time, many Europeans knew the stories about South Americans chewing on coca leaves to increase their energy and decrease their appetite, but no one in Europe had really seen cocaine in action, much less proven the claims with chemistry. Not until sometime between 1855 and 1862 was cocaine identified in the coca leaf and officially described by scientists.

About 10 years after its discovery, Europeans began to recognize the pain-killing abilities of cocaine. Throughout the 1870s and 1880s, scientists studied the effects and potential medicinal uses of cocaine. Around this time the drug company Merck began to produce small amounts of cocaine—less than one pound per year—and sell it to doctors. There wasn't much of a market for the new drug yet.

But good news spreads quickly. By the end of the 1800s, cocaine was widely used in Europe as a cure-all drug. It numbed the skin during painful eye, nose, and

COCAINE AND WINE, COMBINED

In 1863, Frenchman Angelo Mariani created and sold a new beverage: cocaine mixed with wine. He called the tonic "Vin Mariani" and marketed it widely and wisely. Mariani was not a proven scientist, nor was he a doctor—but he was a very good businessman.

Mariani apparently created the cocaine-tainted beverage when working as an assistant in a pharmacy. At the time, medications were often mixed with wine to improve the taste and because medicines dissolved better in alcohol than in water. More than 150 medicinal wines were in use in 1844, so it's not shocking that Mariani, who had read of the miraculous powers of cocaine, thought to add cocaine to wine.

Mariani quit his job and went into business himself. He printed scientific-sounding brochures containing information on the health benefits of his cocaine-tainted wine and gave them away free to doctors. At the same time, he advertised heavily in Paris newspapers, using celebrity endorsements (including the Catholic Pope) in his advertisements. His marketing plan worked. Soon Mariani was selling his product. He also had competitors copying his wine in England and the United States.

Despite its popularity, there is no record of anyone becoming addicted to Vin Mariani. This is likely due to the fact that there really wasn't much cocaine in the wine from the start. Experts estimate that two glasses of Vin Mariani would have contained about 50 milligrams of cocaine.

(continues on page 32)

(continued from page 31)

Vin Mariani advertisements, like this from an 1893 *Harper's Weekly* magazine, boasted the cocaine and wine mixture's ability to serve as a stimulant.

Ingested with wine, 50 milligrams was barely enough to produce a measurable effect in humans.

It is a mystery whether or not Mariani realized the amount of cocaine in his wine was ineffective. Although he always claimed that he was a certified pharmacist in his marketing materials, there is no record that he ever passed the test for certification as a pharmacist. He is often considered the first cocaine millionaire.

throat surgeries; it lifted the mood of depressed patients; it was used to "treat" morphine addiction; and it helped increase the energy levels of athletes.

FREUD ON COCAINE

In 1884, fresh out of medical school at age 28, the young Sigmund Freud published the first and perhaps the most influential scientific paper on cocaine. It was called *Über Coca*, or *On Coca*. The paper got a lot of attention at the time. It also got a lot of things wrong.

On Coca did two things: First, it summarized the work of other researchers in a respectable, reliable way. It is considered the first professional documentation of cocaine's known history and chemistry and was very influential at the time. Second, it went on to recommend the drug for specific medical uses.

This is where Freud took a gamble. At the time, Freud had no experience with cocaine or its effects himself, yet he suggested it as a cure-all medication to treat headaches, bad moods, and other substance addictions. Perhaps most importantly, Freud believed cocaine could be used to treat morphine addiction. In reality, morphine addicts treated with cocaine simply became cocaine addicts as well.

Historians suggest that later in Freud's career, after the harmful effects of cocaine were better understood by science, Freud regretted his public support and prescriptions of cocaine use. Yet he never formally withdrew his initial recommendations for cocaine use.

At the same time, bad news spreads slowly. Soon, Merck was manufacturing cocaine by the ton without anyone really understanding what cocaine was doing in the human body. No one really cared. It would take another hundred years before the harmful effects of cocaine were understood and recognized.

COCAINE IN THE UNITED STATES

As cocaine use and knowledge spread in Europe in the late 1800s, word slowly made its way to the United States. By 1885, the U.S.-based drug manufacturer Parke–Davis was making and selling cocaine commercially. Parke–Davis sold cocaine in cigarettes, powder, and as an injectable mixture.

For the first time, powdered cocaine could be purchased in large quantities in the western world. American winemakers started adding cocaine to their beverages. But unlike the wines sold in Europe, which were flavored with coca leaves, U.S. winemakers added pure, powdered cocaine to their wines. As a result, American wines had a much higher cocaine content.

Because these wines were widely available and purchased, some experts suggest that the drinks helped to quickly make the addictive and damaging powers of cocaine clearer to the general public. By the early 1900s, Americans began to question cocaine use. In 1906, the United States responded by passing the Food and Drug Act, partially to help educate consumers about cocaine content. The act required that the ingredients in foods and medicines be listed on the products' labels. The law was the first step in an ongoing effort to regulate cocaine use and abuse.

But the act wasn't enough. Fewer than 10 years later came the Harrison Narcotics Act of 1914. This law banned cocaine use in medicines and made the drug

A late 19th-century advertisement for Cocaine Toothache Drops promises to cure pain.

illegal for nonmedical, or recreational, use. At this point, cocaine could not legally be added to wines, cigarettes, medicines, or other products sold to the public. Cocaine officially became an illegal drug.

But cocaine use did not go away immediately. By this time, it could be reasoned that many American users—most notably, people in Hollywood—were already addicted to the drug and continued to use it regularly. Cocaine was regularly featured in films until 1922, when 37 states passed laws that prohibited movies showing drug use from being screened locally.

As a result, cocaine use started to decrease in the 1930s. U.S. laws started to get tougher at the same time. The 1961 Single Convention on Narcotic Drugs banned the production and trade of cocaine, opium, and marijuana in the United States. Then the 1970 Controlled

(continues on page 38)

COCAINE AND COCA-COLA

In 1911, the manufacturers of Coca-Cola were sued for two things: poisoning the youth of America with caffeine, and *failing* to add cocaine to their product.

Coca-Cola was originally created as a medicinal drink, promising to cure "nervous trouble, dyspepsia [stomach pain], mental and physical exhaustion, all chronic and wasting diseases, gastric irritability, constipation, sick headache and neuralgia [nerve disorder]," according to *A Brief History of Cocaine*, by Steven B. Karch. To achieve these lofty goals, the original drink, created in 1886, contained lime juice, sugar, citrus oils, cinnamon, coriander, nutmeg, caffeine, and fluids extracted from coca leaves.

Some sources say the Coca-Cola Company purchased as much as 115 tons (104 metric tons) of coca leaf from Peru and 105 tons (95 metric tons) from Bolivia each year to use as flavoring in its beverage. According to the great-grandson of one of Coca-Cola's founders, the original soda formula called for just 10 pounds of coca leaves per 36 gallons of cola syrup. This means that each gallon of Coca-Cola contained just 22.5 milligrams of cocaine—an amount too small to produce any detectable response in the body. So although it's true that Coca-Cola did contain cocaine for more than 20 years, it wasn't enough cocaine to do anything in the body.

Not surprisingly, the medicinal version of Coca-Cola did not sell as planned. But its creators did not give up. Coca-Cola was repackaged with cold, carbonated water and sold to cafes in the South. In this form, it was a normal

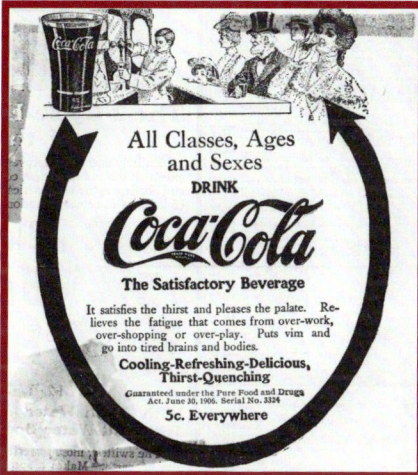

All Classes, Ages
and Sexes

DRINK

Coca-Cola

The Satisfactory Beverage

It satisfies the thirst and pleases the palate. Re-
lieves the fatigue that comes from over-work,
over-shopping or over-play. Puts vim and
go into tired brains and bodies.

**Cooling-Refreshing-Delicious,
Thirst-Quenching**

Guaranteed under the Pure Food and Drugs
Act, June 30, 1906. Serial No. 3324

5c. Everywhere

This early Coca-Cola advertisement encourages men and women to enjoy the beverage and its ability to restore energy to tired brains and bodies.

beverage. The number of potential buyers rapidly increased and sales soared.

At about the same time as Coca-Cola was becoming widespread, the public was learning more and more about cocaine. Cocaine developed a reputation as a drug for the underprivileged, uneducated, and generally menacing members of the population. Coca-Cola, of course, did not want to be associated with such a reputation. So to avoid damaging the sales of Coca-Cola with cocaine, the creators found a way to add the flavor of the coca leaf without adding the cocaine. In 1906, cocaine was removed entirely from Coca-Cola.

Then in 1911, Coca-Cola was sued for false labeling because it did not contain coca and hardly any cola.

(continues on page 38)

(continued from page 37)
The trial took six years to play out. In the end, Coca-Cola reduced the amount of caffeine in its beverage and caffeine was added to the list of dangerous drugs in the Pure Food and Drug Act. The act, established in 1906, ensures that food ingredients are safe and that foods are labeled properly. But cocaine was never again added, and Coca-Cola kept its name.

(continued from page 35)
Substances Act was passed to regulate the manufacture, importation, possession, and distribution of cocaine in the United States. This act is still in effect today.

Yet again, cocaine use did not go away. In fact, cocaine started to become more popular as a recreational drug in the 1970s. Cocaine became a "glamorous drug" during this decade, selling for $100 or more per gram. This meant that only wealthy people could afford to use it. Between 1976 and 1981, cocaine-related medical emergencies and deaths tripled.

By the 1980s, a cheaper version of cocaine, known as crack, became popular among less wealthy people and resulted in more people using these drugs. The U.S. crack epidemic had begun. According to surveys done by the National Institute on Drug Abuse (NIDA), cocaine and crack use by high school students rose from 9% to 17% between 1975 and 1985. NIDA also reported that by 1992, almost 2% of all the babies born in the United

States—known as "crack babies"—had been exposed to some form of cocaine before they were born.

Through the 1980s, the American public became more and more aware of the dangers of cocaine and crack. At the same time, the government increased law enforcement efforts and adopted a zero-tolerance policy for drug use in the military. Over time, the use of cocaine and crack slowly decreased, but it did not go away. Today cocaine remains the second most popular recreational drug sold in the United States; Only marijuana is used more.

3

The Chemistry of Cocaine

Forget, for just a moment, about all the bad things already known about this illegal drug, and take a look at the basic chemistry of cocaine. In the end, it is the specific chemistry of the cocaine **molecule** that makes this drug a drug.

A molecule is a group of chemical substances held together in a specific structure. Exactly which substances are involved and how they are held together in space determines how that molecule behaves in the universe, on the planet, and in the human body.

A molecule of water, for example, freezes at 32°F (0°C) because of its chemical ingredients and its structure. A molecule of sugar gnaws away at your teeth because of its chemical ingredients and its structure.

A molecule of cocaine enters and moves through the body the way it does because of its chemical ingredients and its structure. In the end, the chemistry of cocaine counts.

THE INGREDIENTS OF COCAINE

It may not be obvious to the nonscientist, but the word *cocaine* actually tells a lot about the chemical ingredients of the cocaine molecule. The word *cocaine* is a combination of two words: *coca*, the plant that naturally makes the chemical substance, and *-ine*, a common word ending given to a group of chemical substances known as **amines**.

Amines can be created naturally by plants or animals and are often used as color dyes, additives for gasoline, and as drugs. The leaves of the coca plant, a big, bushy plant with green leaves that is native to northwestern South America, naturally produce the amine known as cocaine.

An amine is a type of molecule with a specific list of chemical ingredients. All amines are made of the element nitrogen (N) and three other groups of elements. An **element** is a substance that cannot be changed into another substance through normal chemical means. Elements are the simplest natural substances in the universe. Everything in the universe is made up of some combination of elements.

The smallest piece of an element that still maintains the properties, or characteristics, of that element is called an **atom**. One atom of the element nitrogen (N) is at the center of all amine molecules. Connected to the central nitrogen atom are three other groups of elements (called "X" here). These can be single elements, such as oxygen (O) or hydrogen (H), or they can be larger groups of elements, such as CH_3. A methylamine, for example, is one N atom bonded to two hydrogens and one CH_3 group (CH_3NH_2). The basic structure of an amine molecule, and the methylamine example, look like this:

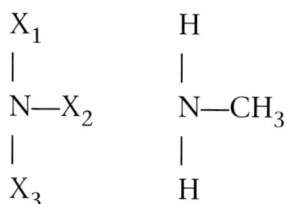

$$
\begin{array}{cc}
X_1 & H \\
| & | \\
N-X_2 & N-CH_3 \\
| & | \\
X_3 & H
\end{array}
$$

Different amines have different groups of connected elements (X), but all have these four basic ingredients: one nitrogen atom plus three "X" groups of elements. The cocaine molecule is actually a rather complex amine with different, complicated "X" groups. It has one nitrogen atom connected to large groups of carbon (C), hydrogen (H), and oxygen (O) atoms. A cocaine molecule looks something like this:

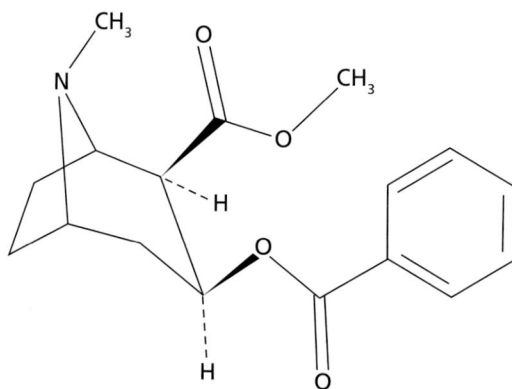

Cocaine

In the image of the cocaine molecule, the nitrogen atom (N) is on the left. It is connected to a simple CH_3

molecule (one of the "X" groups), and two other web-like groups of atoms (the other two "X" groups). In cocaine's case, the "X" groups make cocaine an amine, but the exact ingredients of each group are less important. What makes cocaine an amine is the single nitrogen atom with three groups of elements attached.

Chemists write cocaine using its chemical symbols; it looks like this: $C_{17}H_{21}NO_4$. This means there are a total of 17 carbon atoms, 21 hydrogen atoms, and 4 oxygen atoms connected to a single atom of nitrogen. These are the basic ingredients of the cocaine molecule. But the structure of cocaine can vary. How these ingredients are structured in space impacts how the molecules move and act in the body.

THE STRUCTURE OF COCAINE

Cocaine always contains the same basic chemical ingredients. But those ingredients can be arranged differently in space to create different physical structures. Many people are familiar with the powdery, crystal-like form of cocaine often seen in movies; or perhaps they also know the solid, white, rock-like form, known as crack, which might make the evening news in reports about drug busts.

Each of these unique physical structures is created through chemistry. And each has a defined, predictable organization of elements and atoms inside the molecules. This organization is important because the different varieties enter and act differently in the human body.

Powdered cocaine is probably the most well–known form of this drug. When many molecules of powdered cocaine get together, certain atoms in one cocaine molecule are naturally attracted to the atoms in another cocaine molecule. These atoms "stick" to each

THE COCA PLANT

The coca plant, *Erythroxylum coca,* is a bushy, straight, green plant that can grow up to 10 feet (3 m) tall. It has dark-green leaves that narrow to a point, and small white flowers that turn into bunches of red berries. All together, there are more than a dozen different varieties, or species, of the coca plant. Each has its own characteristics and cocaine content. Some coca plants have more cocaine than others, but all produce the drug when they grow.

All coca plants grow naturally in northwest South America, where the weather is hot, humid, and wet for most of the year. Some varieties grow best on mountainsides exposed to the sun and air, while others prefer the damp forest floor.

The coca leaf is the part of the plant that produces cocaine. The exact amount produced varies, but in general fresh coca leaves contain only about 0.2% pure cocaine, a very small amount. In addition to cocaine content, the coca leaves contain a variety of nutrients, proteins, and vitamins.

Some suggest that South American natives have chewed coca leaves for thousands of years not only for the cocaine side effects, but also for the nutritional value of the leaves when other foods were scarce. When chewed, the leaves have a strong, tea-like taste and make the mouth slightly numb. The cocaine that enters the body acts as a stimulant, keeping a person from feeling hungry, thirsty, or tired.

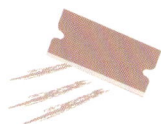

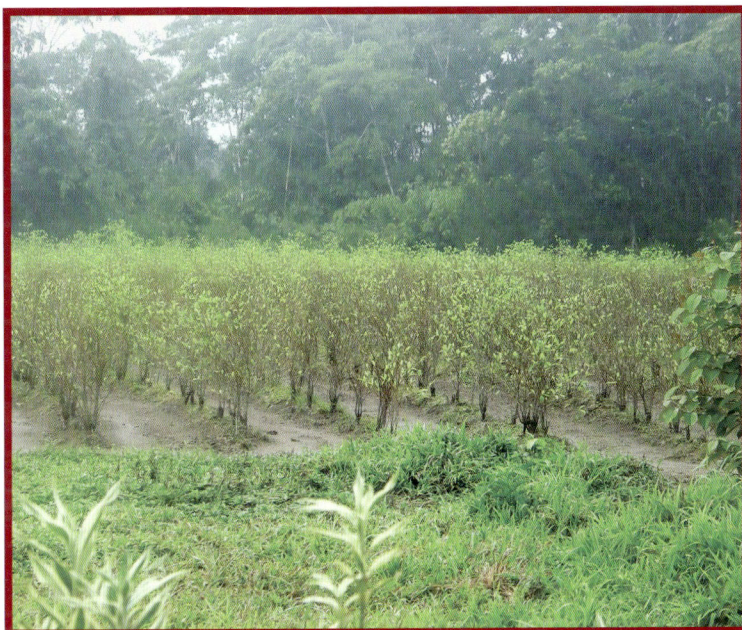

Coca plants are farmed in lines near Cuzco, Peru. Natives in South America have been chewing the leaves for thousands of years. In both Peru and Bolivia, the leaves are used in teas to lessen feelings of altitude sickness.

The cocaine content can be preserved when the leaves are picked and dried in the correct way. The dried coca leaves smell like tea and are commonly shipped in dried form for use in the medical industry and as part of the illegal drug trade.

other in predictable ways. The result is a well-packed, organized, regular pattern of molecules in space. This pattern of packed molecules is what gives this type of cocaine its powdery appearance.

The way molecules stick together is not unlike the way pieces of a puzzle fit together. The end of one puzzle piece fits nicely to the end of another puzzle piece in a specific, predictable way. Once the puzzle pieces are all connected, they produce an organized pattern. In chemistry, such puzzle-piece molecules create what is called *crystalline structures*. A **crystal** is simply a well-packed, well-organized group of molecules.

Powdered cocaine is considered a crystal. It is also considered a salt. In chemistry, **salts** are neutral, uncharged compounds that have common characteristics. All salts have the crystal-like structure and certain chemical ingredients in common. These two basic things make all salts behave in similar ways. Perhaps most important in the case of cocaine is that all salts dissolve easily in water. The blood in your body is made up of more than 90% water. This makes it very easy for powdered cocaine to dissolve in the blood, move through the body, and spread its effects.

The drug can enter the bloodstream in a variety of ways. **Cocaine hydrochloride**, for example, is the chemical name for the powdered salt form of cocaine. It can be eaten or drunk, eventually entering the blood via the digestive system. It can also be inhaled through the nostrils, where it travels into the body through the nose to enter the blood. It can also be mixed with water and injected directly into the bloodstream with a needle.

In each case of entry, the salt structure of cocaine allows it to dissolve easily in blood and move quickly throughout the body. Cocaine hydrochloride, like all salts, is a neutral molecule without any charge. But when salt enters water and dissolves, it breaks into two pieces: one negatively charged and one positively charged.

These charged particles are what make cocaine eager to interact with other molecules. They can easily rearrange themselves into new things or force other molecules to rearrange and change. When cocaine dissolves

DISCOVERY OF THE COCAINE MOLECULE

German chemist Friedrich Gaedcke (1828–1890) was the first person to isolate the cocaine molecule from the coca leaf and publish the results in 1855. He described small crystal molecules with needle-like points on four to six sides, and named the new molecules erythroxyline (after the scientific name of the coca plant, *erythoxylon*). Gaedcke also described the numbing effects of the cocaine molecules when placed on the tongue.

Surprisingly, Gaedcke's work received little attention at the time. No one, it seems, was that interested in the chemistry of cocaine. But within four years, two other chemists repeated Gaedcke's work and came to the same scientific conclusions. This time one of the chemists, Albert Niemann, received a lot of attention.

It wasn't that Niemann discovered anything different—he rediscovered the same things as Gaedcke—but he worked for one of the most famous chemists of the time. As a result, his work received a lot of publicity. By 1862, the drug company Merck began to use Niemann's chemistry techniques to isolate the cocaine molecule from the coca leaf and produce purified cocaine for sale.

Crack is a highly addictive form of cocaine. It became popularized as a drug of abuse in the mid-1980s. Abusers find that the drug produces an immediate high and is inexpensive to produce, which makes it more readily available and affordable than some other drugs.

into its parts, it interacts with other molecules in the body and produces effects in the body—for better or worse.

Crack cocaine is another well-known form of this drug. Crack cocaine is created when powdered cocaine is boiled together with baking soda and water. During boiling, a solid substance, called a **precipitate**, forms and sinks to the bottom of the liquid. This white, rock-like solid is crack.

In chemistry, a precipitate is a solid that forms when molecules in a liquid rearrange themselves to form

FIGURING OUT WHERE COCAINE COMES FROM

Cocaine, it turns out, holds onto chemical clues that reveal where on Earth the drug was originally grown. By studying these chemical clues—sort of like stamps marking the country of birth—law-enforcement officials can determine where batches of illegal drugs came from. This helps officers track down the people who are growing and distributing the drug.

The chemical clues exist because as a coca plant grows, it takes in the elements carbon and nitrogen from the environment. Different environments create different amounts and varieties of carbon and nitrogen in the coca plant. The environment's climate, including the humidity, length of the dry season, and soil chemistry, contribute to the unique chemical signature stamped on the coca plants grown in that area.

For many years, law enforcement officials have "read" these chemical signatures to determine the origins of confiscated cocaine samples. The chemical method of identification is considered quite reliable. In one study, reported in *Science News Online* in 2000, scientists were able to pinpoint the origin of cocaine samples with a 96 percent accuracy rate.

something new. Precipitation is often used in industry to make paint, strengthen metals, and purify liquids. In the illegal drug world, it is used to make crack cocaine.

During the process of precipitating powder cocaine to crack cocaine, the parts of the molecule that make powder cocaine a salt are removed. The salt parts of the cocaine molecule "stick" to the baking soda and remain dissolved in the water, while the pure cocaine becomes a solid precipitate that sinks to the bottom of the liquid. Powdered cocaine is a salt, but crack cocaine is not. This means crack enters and reacts in the body in a very different way than powdered cocaine.

Powdered cocaine dissolves in the blood and breaks into excited, positive and negative charged particles. This chemical breakdown of cocaine means it takes only about 5 to 10 minutes for the user to feel the effects of the powdered drug. This process is fast, but crack is faster. Instead of the two-step process of dissolving and breaking in the blood, solid crack is heated, or smoked, to change it into a gas. Smokers inhale this crack gas directly into their lungs, where it immediately enters the bloodstream as positively and negatively charged, excited particles. It takes only about five seconds for these particles to enter the **brain**. As a result, the effects of smoking crack cocaine are felt very quickly by the user and are often described as more "intense."

Pure cocaine, straight from the coca leaf, is neither a powdery salt nor a crack-like solid. It is a group of molecules organized and packed into crystal-like forms often described as pearly, rather than powdered. Pure cocaine traditionally enters the body through two different routes: chewing and brewing.

Coca leaves have been chewed for thousands of years. They are typically chewed with lime juice, and held in the mouth between the cheek and the gums, like chewing tobacco. Some of the juice is slowly sucked and swallowed, while some is absorbed through the skin of the cheek and into the bloodstream. Cocaine entering the bloodstream through the skin of the cheek can

WHAT TO DO IN PERU

In late 2007, a battle was brewing in the country of Peru, located on the northwestern coast of South America. Government leaders there seem torn between the long-respected virtues, value, and culture of the coca plant, and doing away with illegal coca leaf crops altogether.

Peruvian farmers hold coca leaves as they attend a ceremony at which President of the Cuzco region of Peru, Oscar Cuaresma, signed a new law regarding the plant in June of 2005. Under pressure from the farmers, lawmakers declared coca (the raw material for cocaine) a local treasure. Critics worry that this move was designed to legalize production of the plants.

(continues on page 52)

(continued from page 51)

On one hand, the president of Peru, Alan García, strongly believes in the value of legal coca. The country currently grows coca leaves legally on about 25,000 acres of land, an area almost twice the size of the island of Manhattan in New York. This coca is sold to other countries that use it to produce herbal teas, create pharmaceutical cocaine (the legal, medicinal version of the drug), and make soft drink flavorings. Coca is a legal, valuable exported product. García has also promoted new legal uses for the plant. On one occasion he said coca leaves "can be consumed directly and elegantly in salad."

At the same time, cocaine is illegal and President García promises to get rid of illegal coca crops in his country to assist with the worldwide war on drugs. In December 2006, García promised U.S. President George W. Bush that Peru would continue to battle illegal coca crops. The trick, however, is this: About 90 percent of the cocaine grown in Peru is illegal. And Peru is the second largest cocaine producer in the world, second only to Colombia.

Stopping such a powerful and profitable industry will not be politically popular in Peru. Even the country's leaders admit that it's going to take a lot of work to actually get rid of illegal coca crops in Peru.

produce a slight numbing effect inside the mouth, but in this case there is not enough of the drug to have much effect on the body. When the coca leaves themselves are swallowed, the digestive acids in the stomach break the cocaine molecules apart and make them ineffective as a drug. But when swallowed with something acidic, such as lime juice, the cocaine molecules can avoid breakdown by stomach acids and eventually be absorbed into the bloodstream.

In addition to chewing fresh coca leaves, brewing dried coca leaves in hot water has been practiced for thousands of years. In this case, dried coca leaves (with the pure cocaine preserved inside) are soaked in water to make a tea-like drink. Drinking coca tea does not produce any numbness in the mouth or major effects in the body. Rather, it is supposed to put a person in a better mood. In many places in South America, visitors are greeted with coca tea because it is believed to help with the physical discomfort a foreigner often experiences when traveling from low-lying regions to areas high in the mountains.

The amount of cocaine in chewed coca leaves and brewed coca tea is tiny compared to the powdered and solid forms of the drug. It is also slow to take effect. Ingestion by these methods takes at least 30 minutes to reach the bloodstream. Nevertheless, chewing coca leaves and drinking coca tea are also considered illegal in the United States.

4

Effects on the Body

Cocaine use has both short- and long-term effects on the human body. Almost immediately after using cocaine—anywhere from five minutes to an hour, depending on the dosage and entry into the body—the heart, veins, and lungs speed up their work. The heart rate increases, blood flows faster, and breathing quickens. During the course of years of usage, cocaine takes a physical toll on the body. The chemistry of the brain changes, holes develop in the nose, the heart gets weak, and lung problems develop.

Exactly what happens to the body and when depends largely on how the drug is taken. Cocaine can be smoked, injected, or snorted. Smoking cocaine attacks the lungs; injecting cocaine impacts the heart and veins;

SHORT- AND LONG-TERM EFFECTS OF COCAINE AND CRACK

The effects of cocaine use appear soon after a single use and can disappear within just a few minutes or hours. According to the National Institute on Drug Addiction's (NIDA) *Research Report Series: Cocaine Abuse and Addiction*, the short-term effects of cocaine include:

- Increased energy
- Decreased appetite
- Mental alertness
- Increased heart rate and blood pressure
- Constricted blood vessels
- Increased body temperature
- Dilated pupils

Unlike the seemingly harmless, short-term effects of cocaine use, long-term cocaine use can eventually be fatal. According to the same NIDA research report, the long-term effects of cocaine include:

- Addiction
- Irritability and mood disturbances
- Restlessness
- Paranoia
- Hallucinations in hearing
- Heart, lung, and stomach diseases
- Neurological disorders

and snorting cocaine damages the nose. But regardless of the route of entry to the body, the brain is always affected in some way.

COCAINE AND THE BRAIN

The physical effects of cocaine on the human body begin in the brain. The brain is the body's command and control center. It is where specialized cells receive and send out messages that control everything the body does.

Some of the things controlled by the brain are conscious behaviors such as thinking, reading, talking, and walking. Other things are controlled unconsciously—without the person thinking about them—such as heart rate, breathing, and digestion. These unconscious things are what are most affected by cocaine.

The brain and spinal cord make up the body's **central nervous system**. The central nervous system contains about 100 billion **neurons**, the specialized cells that receive and send messages in the body. Normally, neurons send messages to other neurons by passing specific chemicals back and forth. When cocaine enters the brain, it changes the way these chemical messages move between neurons, and therefore changes the way the brain works.

Neurons use **dendrites**, branch-like tails on a cell, to pass chemicals back and forth. Think of each dendrite as a hand reaching out to receive the chemical message. Once the message is received and processed, a normal neuron pumps the chemical back to the sender. This all happens very quickly—in small fractions of a second—and is happening constantly in the brain.

Stimulants such as cocaine change the way neurons send these chemical messages, or **neurotransmitters**.

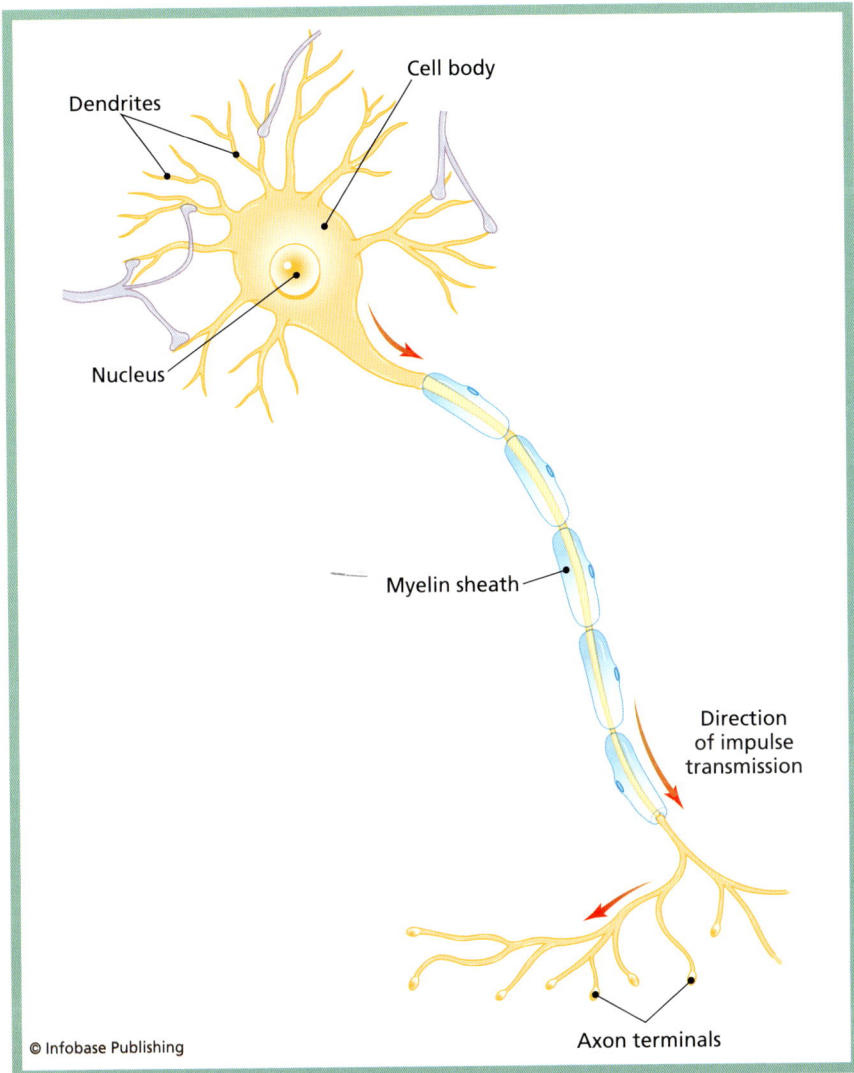

Dendrites

Cell body

Nucleus

Myelin sheath

Direction
of impulse
transmission

Axon terminals

A neuron consists of a cell body, axon, and dendrites. The cell body contains a nucleus, which is the control center of the neuron. Axons carry nerve impulses away from the cell body. They are often wrapped in a fat-soluble layer called myelin, which helps increase the speed of impulse transmission. Dendrites receive nerve impulses from adjacent neurons.

Cocaine prevents the neuron on the receiving end from pumping the neurotransmitter back to the sender. As a result, the neurotransmitter keeps affecting the neuron long after it should have stopped.

All together, there are about 30 different kinds of chemical messages, or neurotransmitters, that are naturally produced by the body. Cocaine strongly affects two specific neurotransmitters: **norepinephrine** and **dopamine**. Each has a very different job in the body.

Norepinephrine's job is to prepare the body for an emergency: to tell cells to get ready for something big. It makes the heart beat faster and increases breathing rate. So when norepinephrine builds up in the brain, the body responds by increasing its heart rate (which increases blood pressure) and by breathing faster.

Dopamine's job is to control feelings of pleasure, to make brain cells "happy." Exactly how this happens is unknown, but when dopamine builds up in the brain the person feels very happy for a short time (often called the "high.") The neurons keep receiving the pleasurable chemical message over and over again.

The norepinephrine and dopamine neurotransmitters are affected immediately when cocaine enters the brain. Over time, this leads to physical changes in the brain. The brain develops a different way of working that requires cocaine to function. At this point, a person is **addicted** to cocaine because he physically needs it for his brain to function.

Cocaine reaches the brain through the blood. All the intake methods—smoking, injecting, and snorting—get cocaine into the blood (and the brain) in one way or another. The drug just takes different routes to get to the brain. At the same time, each intake method has its own unique impact on different parts of the body.

COCAINE + ALCOHOL = COCAETHYLENE

It's probably not news to learn that many cocaine users often drink alcohol while using cocaine. What is news is that there's probably a reason—rooted in the chemistry of the cocaine molecule—for this harmful, addictive behavior.

When cocaine and alcohol are consumed at the same time, an unusual chemical reaction occurs in the body. The elements contained in the cocaine and alcohol molecules rearrange in the liver to form a new substance not normally found in nature. That substance is called **cocaethylene**. In the human body, cocaethylene acts like cocaine to increase energy, improve mood (temporarily), and increase blood pressure and heart rate. But because the cocaethylene molecule is more durable, it does not break down in the body as quickly as cocaine. As a result, it affects the body longer.

Perhaps as a result, many cocaine users drink alcohol while using cocaine. Although users may not fully understand the chemistry behind their actions, they know that it works to enhance the drug's effects. In fact, say scientists at the University of California at Berkeley, the majority of deaths due to cocaine overdoses happen because alcohol is consumed while using the drug.

Furthermore, according to the Berkeley scientists, writing in *Effects of Cocaine and Alcohol Consumption,* cocaine molecules can be detected in the urine of users one to two days after drug use. But cocaethylene molecules are detected in the urine two to four days after drug use, depending on the amount of cocaine and alcohol ingested. This shows that cocaethylene is more durable.

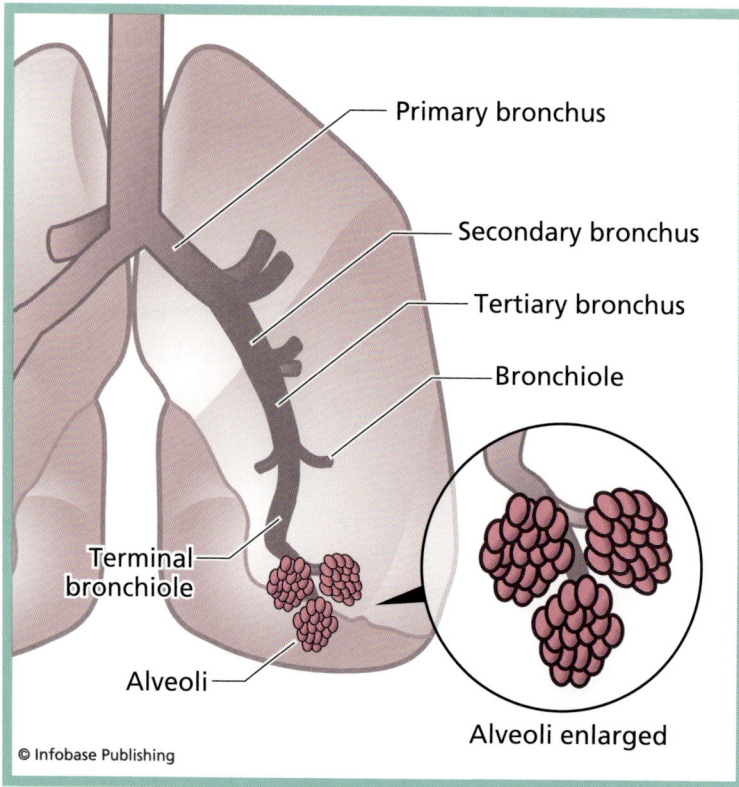

The alveoli are tiny air sacs inside the lungs. When cocaine is inhaled and passes to the lungs, alveoli move the drug into a person's bloodstream.

COCAINE AND THE LUNGS

The lungs branch into many small, root-like tubes with tiny air sacs on the ends called **alveoli**. When breathing normally, the alveoli help transfer inhaled oxygen from the lungs into the bloodstream so that the body can function normally. When cocaine is smoked, the user takes in crack cocaine gas through the nose and mouth and into the windpipe. The crack travels through the windpipe into the lungs. When the smoke hits the lungs, the alveoli help transfer the drug from the lungs into the bloodstream, where it travels straight to the brain.

Smoking crack is sometimes called freebasing because crack is a more pure, basic form of cocaine. Once smoked, crack reaches the brain in about five seconds. A typical crack high is short—no longer than 15 minutes— but intense. As a result, crack is highly addictive because the user is left wanting more once the high is gone.

Over time, smoking crack damages the lungs in different ways. The lungs are lined with hair-like cells called **cilia**, which clean the air before it enters the bloodstream. When that air contains crack, the cilia get very irritated. This irritation can increase the body's heart rate, cause chest pain, make breathing difficult, and cause the lungs to swell. If the lungs swell too much, the person can no longer breathe.

COCAINE AND THE CIRCULATORY SYSTEM

When cocaine is injected into the body with a needle, the drug enters the bloodstream and travels through the veins to all the parts of the body. Body parts designed to absorb blood—such as the heart, lungs, kidneys, and brain—are quickly affected by the cocaine content of the blood. All at the same time, the body experiences increased heart rate, increased breathing, increased pleasure, and overall, an increased cocaine high.

Injection gives the user one of the most powerful and dangerous highs available from cocaine. This is partly because injection is the fastest way to get large amounts of the drug into the body. In addition, when cocaine enters the body, the drug is essentially unprocessed.

When it is inhaled, cocaine is partly filtered by the cilia in the lungs. But when it is injected, pure cocaine goes straight into the body and all its parts.

Because injection is so direct, users and dealers often mix cocaine with other substances to be injected. The added substances, depending on what they are, will either soften or strengthen the impact. Sugar, caffeine,

AIDS AND COCAINE USE

One risk of cocaine use is the increased chance of becoming infected with the virus that causes **AIDS** (acquired immunodeficiency syndrome). AIDS causes the body's immune system (the system that fights off sickness and infection) to stop working. People with AIDS can get sick and even die from illnesses that don't affect healthy people at all.

The only way to get AIDS is through contact with infected blood or infected fluid from sex. Drug users are vulnerable to both, and remain the second largest group at risk for contracting the virus that causes AIDS. They make up about 25% to 30% of the total number of AIDS patients. More often than not, drug users get AIDS by sharing needles and having unsafe sex.

When drug users share needles, a small amount of blood from the first user remains in the needle and can be passed from person to person. When they inject cocaine (or any other drug) with the used needle, users actually inject

flour, and powder are common and cheap mixers that soften the high. Other drugs serve as more expensive mixers that can strengthen the high. A speedball, for example, is a mixture of cocaine and heroin that can produce an extremely strong high.

Over time, injecting cocaine and cocaine mixes causes damage to the heart and veins in a few ways.

a tiny bit of foreign blood as well. If this blood contains the virus that causes AIDS, then the user just gave himself the disease.

At the same time, drug users on a high are less likely to make good decisions about sex. Many experts, including those writing the National Institute on Drug Addiction's *Research Report Series: Cocaine Abuse and Addiction*, suggest that drug addicts are more likely to have unprotected sex with partners who are not well known. Using a condom can prevent the spread of AIDS during sexual contact, but drug users may forget to practice safe sex when high, or may not consider safe sex to be important.

When a person has unprotected sex with someone with AIDS, that person is at a huge risk of contracting the disease. Approximately 30% of all new AIDS cases are women. When and if these women become pregnant and give birth, their newborn babies could also carry the virus that causes AIDS.

The heart is a powerful muscle that pumps oxygen-rich blood to different parts of the body. When cocaine is present, the heart beats faster, and a fast-beating heart is a hard-working heart. If the heart gets too overworked, it can simply stop working. When the heart stops, a person dies.

The veins, which carry blood to the heart, are also at risk. With repeat injections, the veins simply get worn out. When this happens, veins can collapse or get infected and prevent blood flow to the heart. With careless injections, the veins can get clogged with drugs or mixers that do not dissolve properly in the blood. Such clogs can prevent blood from reaching the heart and cause a stroke or heart attack.

COCAINE AND THE NOSE

When cocaine is snorted, users inhale a fine, smooth powder through the nose. Normally, the nose has two jobs: to take in oxygen and to detect smells. In both cases, the incoming air travels through a series of chambers before entering the body's bloodstream. And in both cases, cocaine causes damage.

When the nose takes in oxygen, the oxygen travels into the **nostrils**. The nostrils are two chambers in the nose separated by a cartilage "wall" called the **septum**. Next to each chamber are the **sinuses**, which are air pockets inside the nose. The nostrils and sinuses are both affected when the oxygenated air taken in by the nose contains cocaine.

The sinuses are quickly irritated by cocaine, and irritated sinuses make the nose feel stuffed up, as if the user has a bad cold. At the same time, the inside of the nose and septum dries out, cracks, and bleeds. Eventually, sores can develop on the nose and upper lip. The septum

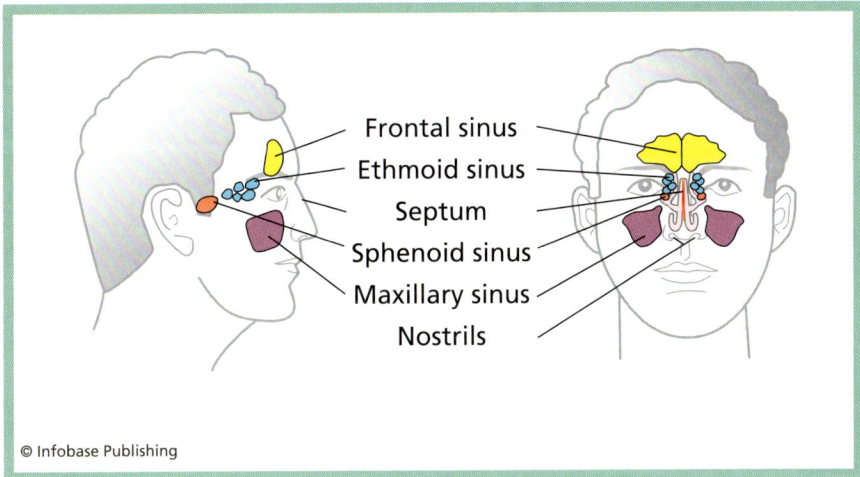

Frontal sinus

Ethmoid sinus

Septum

Sphenoid sinus

Maxillary sinus

Nostrils

Sinuses are air-filled pockets surrounding the nose. There are four types of sinuses on each side of the face. Cocaine irritates the sinuses and interferes with the drainage of mucus, which normally keeps sinuses healthy and moist.

gets weaker with repeated snorting of cocaine, actually developing holes that require surgery to fix.

On top of this, the nose can also lose its ability to smell. Normally when the nose detects a smell, specialized cells inside the nose take in and process the information. But these cells require normal blood flow to stay alive and act as the smelling cells. Cocaine use restricts blood flow to the nose. Eventually the smelling cells—and all the cells that make up the nose—just die. When this happens, the nose basically dies as well.

Because snorted cocaine travels through the different parts of the nose, it takes longer to reach the bloodstream than it does when it is smoked or injected. But as a result of the long route of entry into the body, the high tends to last a little longer as well—up to 30 minutes.

PREGNANCY AND COCAINE USE

When a pregnant woman uses cocaine, she is not only damaging herself—she is also hurting the body and mind of her unborn child. It's not exactly understood what cocaine does to an unborn baby, or how it does it, but each year thousands of "crack babies" are born to drug-using mothers. According to the National Institute on Drug Addiction's *Research Report Series: Cocaine Abuse and Addiction,* some of these babies are often born too soon and with low birth weights. Although some appear to grow

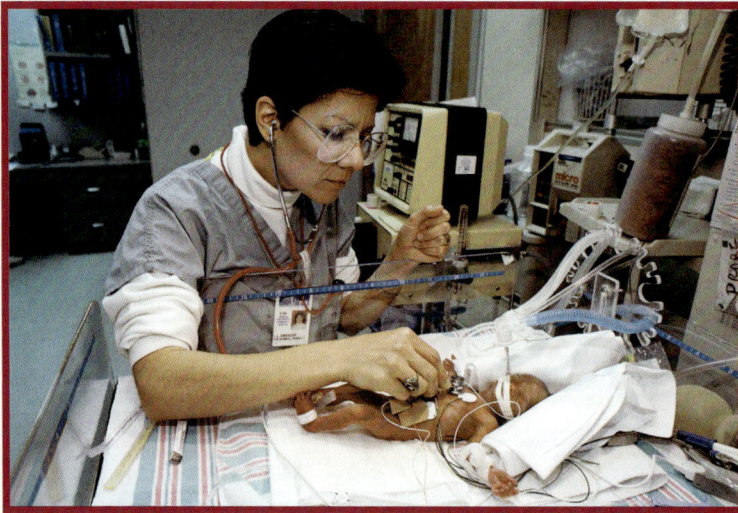

A physician in Washington, DC, checks a premature infant's heartbeat. The tiny baby was born to a woman who went into early labor while smoking crack.

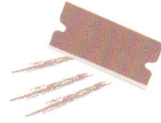

and develop normally, others suffer from permanent and long-term disabilities, including:

- Numerous birth defects and abnormalities (including urinary tract defects)
- Learning disabilities
- Emotional problems
- Problems paying attention
- Poor social skills
- Reduced intelligence

5

Effects on the Mind

The damaged human body is not the only victim of cocaine use. The brain and mind are damaged as well. Here, the general definitions of *brain* and *mind* become important. The brain is the physical, bodily organ contained in the head and all the cells, connections, and chemical processes that happen inside. The **mind**, for the purposes of this book, includes the feelings and actions that result from all the things happening inside the physical brain.

When cocaine changes the brain, it changes the mind as well. No matter how hard an addict tries to be "normal" or stop using cocaine, the physical changes in the brain make the mind feel and act otherwise. Because of this effect, cocaine is considered a very powerful type of stimulant. Once the brain is physically addicted to this stimulant, the mind's escape from this stimulant is not at all easy.

HOW STIMULANTS WORK

Stimulants are drugs that increase physical activity in the body and make a person feel good emotionally. Some stimulants are illegal, such as cocaine and amphetamines (commonly known as "speed.") Other, weaker stimulants are legal, such as caffeine.

Caffeine is a drug commonly contained in foods and beverages, including chocolate, soda, and coffee. Caffeine does the same things to the body and mind as cocaine does, just on a much, much smaller scale.

Like cocaine, caffeine temporarily increases a person's heart rate and breathing. This caffeine high can make consumers feel physically jittery after ingesting this drug. But unlike cocaine, caffeine actually works by increasing the production of dopamine in the brain. Such changes to the brain result in changes to the mind. Because dopamine makes a person feel good, increased dopamine production can make a person feel better. It can also make caffeine consumers feel nervous or energetic after ingesting this widely used and addictive but legal drug.

Cocaine does the same things as caffeine, just on much more severe scale. And caffeine, like cocaine, can be an addicting drug that changes the way the brain works.

COCAINE ADDICTION AND THE BRAIN

Just as high blood pressure is a disease of the heart, addiction is a disease of the brain. A drug addiction occurs when the drug causes physical changes in the

THE BRAIN'S LIMBIC SYSTEM

Although scientists don't yet know all there is to know about the limbic system and how it works, they have figured out the basics. Understanding these basics can go a long way in understanding cocaine abuse and addiction.

The brain's **limbic system** makes and moves dopamine, the neurotransmitter responsible for controlling feelings of pleasure in the brain. When the limbic system is damaged—as it can be by using cocaine—it interferes with how dopamine moves in the brain. As a result, it also interferes with a person's ability to feel pleasure and other emotions. Physically, the limbic system is located at the center of the brain. It includes all the parts of the brain involved in motivation and emotion, plus those that associate smells and feelings.

The limbic system does a lot in a person's day-to-day experiences. When a smell triggers a strong memory, for example, the limbic system is responsible. It also controls things like fear, pleasure, long-term memories, making decisions, and processing thoughts. At the same time, the limbic system influences the **autonomic nervous system**, the parts of the body that work automatically, without thought. This includes things such as heartbeat and blood pressure.

When a person uses cocaine, the drug acts directly on the brain's limbic system and affects all the things that the limbic system controls. For example, a cocaine-affected limbic system can result in the user feeling scared, happy, and depressed all at the same time. The basic role of the brain's limbic system—combined with it being vulnerable to cocaine—explains why the drug impacts a person's emotions, decisions, and bodily processes so strongly.

brain and makes the brain dependent on the drug to work normally. Once the brain is physically changed by a drug, it is very hard to change back.

Cocaine rewires the brain just as an electrician could rewire a television set. Under normal conditions, a television requires electricity to turn on and operate normally. When rewired by an electrician to operate with a different source of power—solar power, for example—the television instead takes in energy from the Sun so that it can turn on and operate normally. It doesn't need electricity anymore, but it does need the Sun. If the weather became very cloudy for a long period of time, the television would not be able to draw power from the Sun, and it would no longer work as it did before. It must be rewired for electricity once again.

Cocaine use rewires the brain in a similar way. Under normal conditions, brain cells pass chemical signals (neurotransmitters) back and forth. When rewired with cocaine, the brain instead pumps neurotransmitters in one direction only. Brain cells that send out neurotransmitters can't take them back anymore. If an addict quits using cocaine, the cocaine goes away but the brain no longer works as it did before.

Addiction occurs because the neurotransmitter dopamine, which is rewired by cocaine, controls feelings of pleasure. With some cocaine use, dopamine builds up in brain cells and makes a person feel very good (the "high.") But with a lot of cocaine use, the brain actually loses its ability to make and move dopamine. As a result, the mind loses its ability to feel good. At this point the brain has been rewired. It can no longer use dopamine "normally" to feel good. Only with cocaine can the brain make and move enough dopamine to feel good. The brain is addicted, requiring cocaine in order to function.

According to scientists at the University of California at San Francisco, it only takes one use of cocaine to rewire the way the brain moves dopamine. The researchers examined changes to the brains of cocaine-treated mice and also found that when the brain is rewired by cocaine, the drug affects all the brain cells, not just a few. This is a surprise, the researchers said,

SIGNS AND SYMPTOMS OF COCAINE ADDICTION

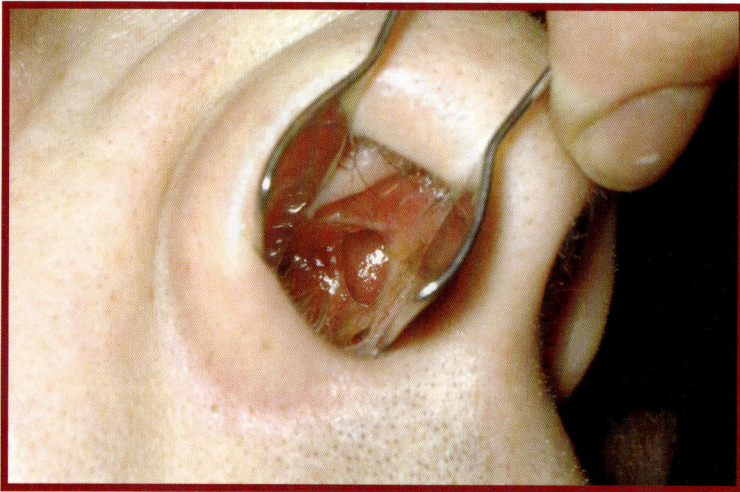

This photograph shows inside the nose of a person who has a perforated nasal septum. The hole is a common symptom of cocaine abuse.

Cocaine is so powerful that a single use can cause a person to become addicted to the drug. According to the Mayo

because usually when the brain learns something new, just a few brain cells are affected. But with cocaine, all the cells that move dopamine are affected at the same time from a single use of the drug. The scientists reported that this likely has a strong effect in areas all over the brain, especially in other parts of the brain that play a role in addiction.

Clinic, a large and respected organization of doctors and health care providers, the general signs and symptoms of cocaine addiction include:

- Euphoria (an intense state of happiness)
- Decreased appetite
- Rapid speech
- Irritability
- Restlessness
- Depression as the drug wears off
- Nasal congestion and damage to the nose in users who snort the drug
- Insomnia (inability to fall asleep)
- Weight loss
- Increased heart rate, blood pressure, and temperature
- Paranoia

As a result, researchers suggest, a person might become addicted to cocaine after just a single use of the drug. The way the brain makes and moves dopamine is significantly altered; and the person's mind is altered as well.

COCAINE ADDICTION AND THE MIND

Once a person's brain is physically addicted to a drug such as cocaine, the mind controls how that person acts and feels with and without the drug. The mind of a drug addict makes the user do everything he or she can to get more of the drug he or she needs to feel "normal." At this point, the drug addict craves the drug. A **craving** is an intense, almost irresistible urge to use a drug. This urge strongly overrides any danger-ous or harmful actions that a normal mind will usually prevent.

Experts at the Mayo Clinic say that when a person is addicted to cocaine or any other drug, the mind tells the body to do very specific things. Addiction can make people feel that they need to:

- Take the drug regularly or many times a day
- Maintain a supply of the drug
- Do things they normally wouldn't do, such as steal things or hurt others
- Take the drug to deal with problems in life
- Drive or do other dangerous activities while under the influence of the drug

Mayo Clinic experts say that an addiction to any drug—not just cocaine—can cause these thoughts and feelings. But with a very powerful drug, such as cocaine, these effects tend to be very strong. The mind is unable to fight off such urges once cocaine has physically changed the brain.

As a result, many scientists and U.S. government agencies have explored how to create medicines to help cocaine addicts stay in control of their actions. They are searching for a medicine that can help a person physically fight the feelings of cocaine cravings. Such

UNDERSTANDING HOW THE BRAIN CONTROLS CRAVINGS OF THE MIND

Changes in the way the brain handles dopamine, the pleasure-controlling chemical in the brain, have been found in rats that have a strong craving for cocaine. Researchers at the University of Texas Southwestern Medical Center examined the cells responsible for moving dopamine in the brains of rats addicted to cocaine. They found that after the rats became addicted to the drug and were then forced to quit, their cells responded differently. Addicted rats were easily persuaded to seek out more cocaine. But because of the physical changes in the brain, the rats were not so easily satisfied by the drug when they got it.

Dr. David Self, one of the authors of the study, said that he and his fellow researchers found biological changes that explain the changes in behavior of cocaine addicts. "It really shows that the addicted person is ill-equipped to cope, because the brain is now wired to make them crave drugs more and get less satisfaction out of the drug or other life events that may be rewarding," he reported in an article in *Medical News Today*.

medications are already marketed to help people stop smoking cigarettes and combat addiction to nicotine, the addictive drug in cigarettes. Effective cocaine medications are still being explored.

Some of these early cocaine medicines can make drug addicts feel unpleasant when they use cocaine. For example, researchers from the National Institute on Drug Abuse tested the drug disulfiram and found that it reduced cocaine use from 2.5 to 0.5 days per week on average. Disulfiram is a well-established medicine used to treat alcoholism, but it works to make cocaine addicts feel restless, anxious, and paranoid when they use cocaine.

Other cocaine drugs change the way dopamine moves in the brain so that cocaine cravings aren't so strong. For example, researchers from the National Institute on Drug Abuse tested the drug topiramate and found that it helped cocaine addicts stay off the drug for three weeks or more. Topiramate is a drug currently used to treat seizures.

Despite these early successes in cocaine medications, there is no magic pill yet to make cocaine addiction go away. No medications are widely available at this time. Instead, the physical symptoms of cocaine addiction are often treated with counseling and group support.

COCAINE WITHDRAWAL

Once addicted to a drug, the brain requires that drug to function normally. When the drug is not available, the addict experiences **withdrawal**. Withdrawal is the experience of uncomfortable physical and/or mental feelings that occurs when a person stops using a drug.

According to *MedlinePlus,* the online encyclopedia from the U.S. National Library of Medicine and the National Institutes of Health, symptoms of cocaine

CAN COCAINE CAUSE DEPRESSION?

Scientists have long known that there is some connection between cocaine addiction and depression—cocaine addicts tend to be depressed—but they haven't pinpointed exactly why. A 2003 study published by scientists at the University of Michigan helps explain this.

Researchers studied the brains of deceased people who had been heavy cocaine users. The scientists found that the brain cells that make and move dopamine, the neurotransmitter that controls feelings of pleasure, were damaged or broken. These missing brain cells could mean that the person is simply physically unable to feel good, that the brain just can't produce feelings of pleasure anymore.

The question, researchers said, is what happens first: Do depressed people start using cocaine to experience a high and feel better, only to eventually become more depressed? Or do cocaine users become depressed because they damage their brains with repeated drug use and prevent the body from physically feeling pleasure?

The answers to these questions cannot yet be determined. But the University of Michigan study did find that more brain damage was present in people who had been severely depressed when they were alive. There is, it seems, still much to be learned.

withdrawal begin almost immediately after cocaine use has stopped. Symptoms can include severe cocaine cravings, in addition to the following:

- Depressed mood
- Tiredness
- General feelings of discomfort
- Vivid and unpleasant dreams
- Agitation and restless behavior
- Slowing of daily activities or not doing anything at all
- Increased appetite

These withdrawal symptoms can last for many months and lead to suicidal thoughts in some addicts. Unlike withdrawal from heroin or alcohol, however, cocaine withdrawal produces no physical effects such as vomiting or shaking. Withdrawal from cocaine happens entirely in the mind. The only way to prevent the symptoms of cocaine withdrawal, according to *MedlinePlus*, is to avoid cocaine use in the first place.

6

Use of Cocaine

Given everything cocaine can do to harm the body and the mind, it's not easy to explain why people use cocaine in the first place. But they clearly do. Some may try cocaine out of curiosity. Some try it to rebel and be "different," and others do it to fit in and make friends.

But one "try" of cocaine can lead to many more problems than the user ever intended. Because the drug is so powerful, addiction happens fast. And even though a user may not intend to damage his or her body and mind with a cocaine addiction, one "try" of cocaine can quickly become a problem beyond her control.

As a result, the U.S. government asserts some control over the availability of cocaine in this country. The United States first made cocaine illegal in 1914 in an effort to protect people from the many problems associated with its use. But by this time, there were already plenty of cocaine addicts hungry for more drugs. In the decades that followed cocaine's ban, an entire industry developed to get cocaine (and other drugs) into this country illegally, to keep addicts supplied with cocaine. Cocaine is big business.

COCAINE DETECTED ON FOREIGN MONEY

The United States isn't the only country with a widespread cocaine problem. People in other countries use it, too, and there's proof: Scientists have discovered that the paper money used in some foreign countries, including Ireland, England, and Spain, often carries traces of cocaine. The powdered form of cocaine easily sticks to the cotton fibers that make up the paper money, and researchers have been surprised by how easy it is to find bills tainted with the drug.

In January 2007, the British Broadcasting Corporation (BBC) reported the results of one study completed at Dublin's City University in the Republic of Ireland. Researchers tested 45 banknotes for cocaine and detected the drug on every bill tested. In fact, some bills had such high levels of cocaine that scientists speculate they were actually rolled up like a straw and used to snort the drug. Interestingly, the study also found that larger bills—including the 20 and 50 euro notes (the equivalent of about 25 and 65 U.S. dollars)—were more likely to contain larger amounts of cocaine.

By the 1970s cocaine use peaked in the United States. Today, all evidence shows that cocaine use and abuse has declined, but is still very much a problem. According to many national sources and surveys, cocaine is still the second most popular recreational drug in the country, after marijuana.

To fight such widespread use and abuse, the United States spends billions of dollars each year to fight the importation, sale, and use of cocaine. According to the Department of Justice's Drug Enforcement Agency (DEA), tens of thousands of people are arrested in the United States each year on cocaine-related charges, and as much as 220 pounds (100 kg) of cocaine are seized each year by federal authorities. So despite law enforcement efforts, cocaine is clearly getting into the country and getting used.

GETTING COCAINE

Getting cocaine into the United States, it seems, isn't that hard—even for teenagers. According to the Monitoring the Future research project, an ongoing study funded by the National Institute on Drug Abuse, young people find it easy to get cocaine if they really want it. The survey results indicate that 20.2% of eighth graders, 30.7% of tenth graders, and 42.5% of twelfth graders said powdered cocaine was "fairly easy" or "very easy" to obtain.

Although the survey did not ask where these young people get cocaine, the U.S. Drug Enforcement Agency says most of the cocaine sold in the United States is brought in from Mexico. In past decades, much of the cocaine in the United States came from South American countries—mainly Colombia and Peru. But in recent years, Mexican drug dealers have largely taken control of the cocaine trade in the United States. In 2005, for

This tiny package is called a wrap sheet deal of cocaine. It contains approximately 0.5 grams of the drug.

example, DEA offices in New York reported that Mexican drug dealers had replaced Columbian drug dealers as the main sources of cocaine in New York City. The DEA also suggests that Mexican dealers' control of cocaine is growing.

Cocaine is sold in nearly every large and mid-size city in the United States, but a few large cities serve as the main distribution centers. In most of these cities, organized gangs of dealers control the distribution of cocaine. But in smaller cities, there are local, independent cocaine dealers as well.

The cost of cocaine and crack from gangs and dealers varies depending on where in the country they are

(continues on page 85)

COCAINE BY ANY OTHER NAME

By now the terms *cocaine* and *crack* are familiar in popular culture. But these drugs have many slang names that are not necessarily recognizable. Below is a list of some common terms for cocaine, crack, and combinations of cocaine with other drugs, in addition to terms for people and things related to these drugs.

SLANG TERM	DEFINITION
51	Combination of crack with marijuana or tobacco
Aspirin	Powdered cocaine
Banano	Marijuana or tobacco cigarettes laced with cocaine
Base	Short for "freebase," as in crack
Bazooka	Combination of crack and marijuana
Beam me up Scottie	Cocaine and PCP
Belushi	Cocaine and heroin
Bingers	Crack addicts
Black rock	The leftovers in a crack pipe
Blanca	Spanish for cocaine
Blanco	Spanish for cocaine plus heroin
Blow	To inhale cocaine
C & M	Cocaine and morphine
Cabello	Spanish for cocaine
Candy sticks	Marijuana cigarettes laced with cocaine
Coke or cola	Cocaine
Dynamite	Cocaine and heroin

(continues on page 84)

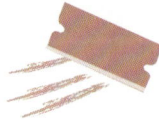

(continued from page 83)

SLANG TERM	DEFINITION
Electric Kool-Aid	Street name for crack
Fast white lady	Powdered cocaine
Flake	A high-quality form of cocaine
G-rock	1 gram of rock cocaine
Gold dust	Powdered cocaine
Horn	To inhale cocaine
Lace	Cocaine and marijuana
Monos	Spanish for a cigarette made from cocaine and tobacco
Nose candy	Cocaine
One bomb	100 rocks of crack
Oolies	Marijuana laced with crack
Powder	The powdered form of cocaine
Real tops	Street name for crack
Rock	Street name for crack
Roxanne	Street name for crack
Snow	Can mean cocaine, heroin, or speed
Snowball	Cocaine and heroin
Soda	Injectable cocaine
Speedball	Cocaine and heroin
Talco	Spanish for cocaine
Toot	To inhale cocaine
Tornado	Crack
Twinkie	Street name for crack
White	Cocaine
Wicky stick	PCP, marijuana, and crack
Yam	Street name for crack

(continued from page 82)
headquartered, in addition to the quality of the drugs. According to the Office of National Drug Control Policy's (ONDCP) *Drug Facts: Cocaine*, 1 gram of powdered cocaine (about enough for 5 to 10 doses of the drug) usually sells for $100 in most cities. But this varies widely.

In New York City, for example, the ONDCP says powdered cocaine ranges from $25 to $35 per gram. In Detroit, however, it sells for $75 to $150 per gram. Some of these differences may be due to other things being mixed with the powdered cocaine to lower the price. Caffeine, chalk, laundry detergent, rat poison, meat tenderizer, and baby powder are all substances that can be mixed with powdered cocaine before it is sold.

Crack cocaine is a little different. A 0.2-gram piece of crack (about enough for one dose) usually sells for $10, says the ONDCP. But this can vary from $2 to $40, depending on the actual size of the rock. Crack is often sold in inner-city areas, while powdered cocaine is sold in both cities and suburban areas.

USING COCAINE

To figure out exactly who uses cocaine in the United States, the federal government has conducted multiple large research studies and surveys. The results of these studies are important because they help explain how big the cocaine problem is in this country. Comparisons of such studies from year to year help explain how the cocaine problem is growing, shrinking, and moving.

The two most recent studies are the 2005 *National Survey on Drug Use and Health* (NSDUH) from the federal Substance Abuse and Mental Health Services Administration (SAMSHA), and the *Monitoring the Future* (MTF) study, funded by the National Institute on Drug Abuse.

The recent NSDUH study helps explain the size of the cocaine problem in the United States. According to the NSDUH, in 2005 about 2.4% of Americans age 12 and older said they used cocaine in the past year. This is much lower than rates for marijuana use—10.6% of Americans in this age group used marijuana in the last year. But the rate for cocaine is higher than usage rates for methamphetamines (0.6%) and heroin (0.2%).

The ongoing MTF study helps explain cocaine use among young people, and how that use has changed in recent years. Since 1975, groups of students in the eighth, tenth, and twelfth grades, plus college students and young adults, have been asked the same set of questions about their use of illegal drugs including cocaine, marijuana, methamphetamines, and others. The goal is to see how drug use changes as the students get older.

According to this study, cocaine use among teens went down slightly in 2006. In 2005, about 3.7% of eighth graders, 5.2% of tenth graders, and 8.0% of twelfth graders reported using cocaine at some point in their lives. In 2006, about 3.4% of eighth graders, 4.8% of tenth graders, and 8.5% of twelfth graders reported using cocaine at some point in their lives.

The study results also pointed out that all ethnic groups and both sexes use cocaine. There is no one group of teenagers more likely to use cocaine than another.

Compared to other countries in the world, Americans use a lot of cocaine. The United Nations Office on Drugs and Crime's *2006 World Drug Report* says the United States has the world's greatest rate of cocaine consumption by people aged 15 to 64, at 2.8%. The United States is closely followed by Spain with 2.7%, and the United

COCAINE FACTS AT A GLANCE

The U.S. government has spent a lot of money to better understand who uses cocaine in this country. Each federally funded study uses slightly different methods to obtain slightly different statistics. Taken together, they provide a picture of current cocaine use in this country.

FACT	REPORT
Overall lifetime use among teens of any illegal drug decreased slightly in 2006. (In 2006 about 21% of 8th graders, 36% of 10th graders, and 48% of 12th graders reported taking an illegal drug in their lives.)	*Monitoring the Future*, from the National Institute on Drug Abuse and the University of Michigan Survey Research Center
Overall, lifetime use among teens of cocaine decreased slightly in 2006. (In 2006 about 3.4% of 8th graders, 4.8% of 10th graders, and 8.5% of 12th graders reported using cocaine in their lives.)	*Monitoring the Future*, from the National Institute on Drug Abuse and the University of Michigan Survey Research Center
2.4% of Americans age 12 and older said they used cocaine in 2005.	*2005 National Survey on Drug Use and Health*, from the Substance Abuse and Mental Health Services Administration (SAMSHA), Department of Health and Human Services
There were an estimated one million new cocaine users in 2004.	*InfoFacts*, from the National Institute on Drug Abuse

(continues on page 88)

(continued from page 87)

FACT	REPORT
Reports from local medical examiner data named Texas and Philadelphia as sites with the highest rates of cocaine-related deaths from 2003 through 2004.	*InfoFacts*, from the National Institute on Drug Abuse
Between 1992 and 2002, the number of people admitted to hospitals mainly because of cocaine problems decreased in 28 states.	*The DASIS Report*, from the Drug and Alcohol Services Information System of the Substance Abuse and Mental Health Services Administration
In 2006, 5,841 people were sentenced for powder cocaine-related charges and 5,623 were sentenced for crack cocaine charges in the United States.	*Drug Facts*, from the Office of National Drug Control Policy

Kingdom with 2.4%. According to the report, most Western European countries have a cocaine consumption rate between 1% and 2%.

STOPPING COCAINE
Each year, the United States spends billions of taxpayer dollars to combat illegal drug use in this country, including illegal cocaine use. For example, in 2000, the most recent year for which statistics are available, the

United States spent about $36 billion fighting cocaine alone. Much of this money is spent on law enforcement at the national level.

Each year the U.S. Drug Enforcement Agency arrests tens of thousands of people on drug-related charges. In 2004, for example, the DEA arrested 27,053 people in the United States. Of these, more than 10,000 were cocaine- or crack-related arrests. While the general law enforcement statistics for cocaine and crack are often lumped together, the individual legal penalties for cocaine and crack are actually quite different.

If a person is arrested for the first time for possessing any amount of powdered cocaine, for example, the maximum amount of time they can spend in jail is one year. But if a person is arrested for the first time for possessing just five grams of crack, the minimum amount of time they can spend in jail is five years. In general, the legal penalties for crack users are much tougher than the legal penalties for cocaine users with no clear explanation of the difference. This seeming inconsistency in the law has prompted lots of debate and discussion. But in most cases, people are arrested for the importation and sale of drugs on a global scale, rather than for individual drug use.

To enforce drug laws on such a huge, global scale, the DEA often cooperates with other organizations and law enforcement agencies. The DEA's Southwest Border Initiative (SWBI) is a good example. The SWBI is a joint effort of the DEA, the FBI, the U.S. Customs Office, and the U.S. Attorneys Office to fight all levels of drug importation and sales along the U.S. border with Mexico. The SWBI targets the communications systems of drug dealers along the border in order to identify and end illegal operations.

Members of the U.S. Coast Guard stand near packages of cocaine, seized last month off the coast of Panama, in Alameda, California on April 23, 2007. The Coast Guard unloaded almost 20 tons of cocaine with a total retail street value of $600 million into the port, following what they said was the largest drug bust ever at sea.

The DEA State and Local Task Force Program also runs local offices throughout the country that work with state and local law enforcement officials to fight the cocaine trade. In New York City, for example, the DEA's New York Task Force works with city and state police officers to enforce the laws. The Task Force also provides funding and extra pay to local law enforcement agencies to insure the job gets done.

OPERATION JOURNEY

Operation Journey was a two-year mission of the DEA and other federal agencies to combat the importation of cocaine. The main target was an organization that imported large amounts of cocaine from Colombia into 12 countries in North America and Europe, including the United States. The drug organization operated 8 to 10 large ships able to haul huge loads of cocaine anywhere in the world by sea. The Colombian cocaine organization owned some of the ships, while groups in other countries owned others.

Cocaine would be loaded onto the ships at ports in Colombia and the nearby country of Venezuela. Once on board, the cocaine was concealed in secret compartments specially built to smuggle drugs. Then the ships set sail. When a ship neared its destination, smaller, faster boats would meet the ship offshore and all the cocaine would be unloaded to these sneakier vessels. The smaller boats would then carefully ferry the illegal cargo to its destinations, successfully sneaking past the country's boarders unnoticed.

For two years, drug enforcement authorities from 12 countries on three continents worked together to break down this organization. When Operation Journey ended in August 2000, a total of 40 individuals had been arrested and more than 16 tons (14.5 metric tons) of cocaine had been seized, worth nearly $1 billion. Among those arrested were the alleged leader of the Colombian cocaine organization, Ivan de la Vega, and many of his employees.

7

How to Find Help

Becoming a cocaine addict is fast and easy. It only takes one use of the drug—in any amount or form—to chemically change the way the brain works and to make the user physically dependent on cocaine to feel normal again.

Becoming a recovered cocaine addict is slow and hard. Very few people can stop using cocaine on their own without some sort of help. And the process does not happen overnight. Teaching the brain to function again without cocaine can take weeks, months, or, in many cases, years.

As hard as it is to stop using cocaine, it is entirely possible. There are few reliable statistics on the success rates of recovering cocaine addicts, but it is true that many people have stopped using cocaine and returned to normal, happy lives. The trick is figuring out when and where to get help for a cocaine addiction and then taking action.

Cocaine addicts don't always realize that they are addicted to the drug and that they need help or treatment. Sometimes it takes an outside voice—a friend or family member, for example—to bring up the problem and perhaps help the addict begin the recovery process.

Although the recovery process is not going to be the same for every addict, there are some general beginning steps that can lead in the right direction. There is a lot to do, but it can be broken down into manageable pieces. The six steps below are not a guarantee of success; nor are they a complete and fool-proof plan for everything that needs to be done. The following outline is, however, a place to start. At times beating a cocaine addiction might seem impossible, but it's not. Start with these steps:

Step 1: Look for behaviors
Step 2: Look for physical signs
Step 3: Consult an expert
Step 4: Ask and admit
Step 5: Make contact
Step 6: Start treatment

STEP 1: LOOK FOR BEHAVIORS

A person who is addicted to cocaine will likely behave in a certain way. Behavior is the way a person acts, feels, and speaks. Sometimes certain behaviors—or sudden changes in behaviors—can be the first warning signs of a cocaine problem.

Many of the behaviors related to cocaine addiction are considered compulsive. A **compulsive behavior** is an action that a person is unable to control due to mental or physical problems. An example might be scratching the skin a lot and always moving and jerking in some way. In many cases, a person engaging in compulsive behaviors does not even realize he is doing anything odd. But it is usually obvious to others.

But odd behavior is not unique to cocaine addiction. A person addicted to heroin or alcohol or some other drug could exhibit some of these same compulsive behaviors. So do not jump to conclusions of cocaine addiction based on behavior alone. Just use them as a place to start.

The behaviors listed below could be early warning signs of cocaine addiction. Look at the suspected person closely. If the person exhibits just one of these behaviors, it may not mean much at all. But if the person exhibits many or all of these behaviors, it may be time to move on to Step 2. Behaviors possibly related to cocaine addiction include:

- Getting high or drunk on a regular basis
- Lying about the amount of alcohol and drugs consumed
- Avoiding old friends (or those that don't do drugs and alcohol)
- Stopping activities (such as sports, hobbies, and homework)
- Constantly talking about drugs and alcohol
- Pressuring other people to do drugs and alcohol
- Needing drugs and alcohol to have fun
- Taking big risks, such as having unprotected sex or driving while under the influence of drugs and/or alcohol
- Feeling tired, hopeless, depressed, or suicidal
- Missing school

- Selling belongings to get extra money for cocaine
- Hanging out with new friends or unknown people
- Getting angry or violent toward objects such as furniture and walls
- Staying awake for very long periods of time
- Sleeping for very long periods of time

COCAINE PSYCHOSIS

Some cocaine users develop a mental illness known as **cocaine psychosis**. People with this problem often see, hear, and feel things in an abnormal way. They might also hallucinate—see, hear, and feel things that simply are not there.

In some cases, for example, a person with cocaine psychosis feels as if there are insects crawling under his or her skin. The person will scratch the skin violently—to the point of drawing blood—to remove the imaginary bugs. Other people might hear voices that aren't there, or might be followed by violent dogs that don't exist, or might see swirling white snakes that no one else can see.

The trick with cocaine psychosis is that the user is not aware that cocaine is causing the distorted senses. Other drugs can cause similar hallucinations, but the user is usually aware that the drug is to blame. As a result, people with cocaine psychosis may be afraid, confused, or violent when such hallucinations happen. They don't realize that cocaine is the culprit.

STEP 2: LOOK FOR PHYSICAL SIGNS

A person who is addicted to cocaine will likely show physical signs of addiction. Physical signs include different characteristics of appearance and general health. Sometimes certain physical signs or changes can be warning signs of a cocaine problem.

The stereotypical image of a drug addict is a skinny, pale, sickly-looking person who appears as though he or she could break into two pieces at any moment. Such images have been popularized in fashion magazines and movies, but they are not at all healthy. Such an appearance can be a strong physical sign of a drug problem.

As with the behaviors sometimes associated with cocaine use, however, certain physical signs are not a guarantee of cocaine addiction. A person addicted to other drugs can exhibit the same or similar physical characteristics. And in many cases, a cocaine addict will not use only cocaine. It is likely he or she uses other drugs and alcohol, too. On the other hand, a person with no drug problem at all might have physical symptoms that may look like cocaine addiction, such as sweating and severe headaches.

Use the physical signs listed below as possible indicators of cocaine addiction. Again, look at the suspected person closely. One physical sign may not mean anything. But if the person exhibits many or all of the physical signs, it may be time to move on to Step 3. Physical signs possibly related to cocaine addiction include:

- Wide-open pupils, even in bright places, which may be covered up by wearing sunglasses constantly
- High body temperature, sweating, and complaints of being hot all the time
- Severe headaches

- Dry mouth
- Shaking hands, fingers, or other body parts
- Dizziness
- Rapid breathing
- Increased heart rate
- Unconsciousness
- Extreme weight loss
- Pale skin

COCAINE ANONYMOUS

If help is needed, Cocaine Anonymous (CA) can provide it. CA is an international organization of men and women with the same goal: to recover from cocaine addiction. There are no dues or fees to become a member. The only requirement is a desire to stop using cocaine. The treatment program at CA is modeled after the widely successful program Alcoholics Anonymous (AA). CA uses a similar Twelve Step Recovery Program (available online at http://www.ca.org/12and12.html) to treat any form of cocaine use and abuse—for example, injecting, snorting, and smoking crack.

To become a member and start the treatment program, cocaine users simply need to find and attend a meeting in their area. According to the group's Web site, there are about 2,000 meetings each week in the United States and Canada, with more starting regularly in Europe. The meetings are conducted independently, with no ruling organization telling local meeting leaders or members what to do.

- Decaying or discolored teeth
- Scars on the skin, possibly from scratching at imaginary bugs or from needle injections.

STEP 3: CONSULT AN EXPERT

If a person exhibits many of the behavioral and physical signs of cocaine addiction, get a second opinion immediately. A good friend may be too close or too difficult to really evaluate alone. Another person—with an open mind—can sometimes help.

Make a simple list of the warning signs observed and take it to a trusted adult or expert. Talk to a trusted person. Explain the reasons for concern, and ask the person what he or she thinks. If the person is a teacher, coach, or family member, he or she may be able to make recommendations on what to do next. If the person is a doctor or counselor trained in drug addiction, he or she might be able to get directly involved.

If there really isn't a trusted person that can make recommendations or get involved with a person possibly addicted to cocaine, there are many other resources out there. Consult one of these free resources if other options are not available. Like a trusted person, these resources may be able to offer recommendations on what to do next.

Call a cocaine hotline. A hotline is a place to call for help. Many hotlines are open all day, everyday, and are staffed by people trained to help with specific problems. There are alcohol hotlines, suicide hotlines, eating disorder hotlines, drug addiction hotlines, and many, many more. Large cities likely have local hotlines specializing in cocaine addiction—just look them up in the phone book—but national hotlines work just as well in most cases.

Visit a city or local health department. Most health departments will have free resources on drug addiction, plus information on where to go in the area for more help. If there are any support groups, counseling centers, or meeting places for cocaine addicts, the health department may be able to point the way.

Find a local support group. Support groups are places where people with similar problems meet and talk.

COCAINE RECOVERY RESOURCES AT A GLANCE

The following organizations can provide information and help in dealing with cocaine and crack.

ORGANIZATION	WEB SITE	PHONE NUMBER
Cocaine Anonymous	www.ca.org	1–800–347–8998 to find a meeting
Cocaine and Crack Cocaine Addiction	www.cocainedrugaddiction.com	1–800–784–6776 help hotline
Cocaine Help	www.cocainehelp.org	none available
Cocaine Help Line	www.coolnurse.com	1–800-COCAINE help hotline
Cocaine Hotline	www.cocainehotline.com	1–800-NODRUGS help hotline
Crack Cocaine Addiction Recovery Support	www.crackcocainerecovery.com	none available
Smart Recovery	www.smartrecovery.org	1–866–951–5357 to find a meeting

Although a person suspected of cocaine addiction probably isn't yet ready to attend a support group meeting, it may be helpful to go to a meeting and see if there are any experts or recovering cocaine addicts who can help.

Go to a hospital or emergency health clinic. Hospitals and health clinics often employ people trained to treat a variety of health problems, including drug addictions. If a cocaine addiction is strongly suspected, some clinics might provide free, professional help. At the very least, someone at a hospital or clinic can recommend where to go next.

STEP 4: ASK AND ADMIT

So far, much of what has been discussed here about how to help a person addicted to cocaine is basic research and information gathering: learning the behavioral and physical warning signs, then confirming with an adult, expert, or other source what those signs might mean. If a cocaine addiction is still suspected, it's time to confront the person.

But be careful in this step. Confronting a person about cocaine use is a serious task. Don't confront the person by accusing him or her of having a problem. This will likely just make the person defensive and start a big argument. Instead, wait for a good time, when the person is not high, and ask if he or she has a cocaine problem. Express any concerns slowly and sincerely. Talk about any worries, fears, and pain that have occurred. Keep the focus off the cocaine addict, and talk in terms of what's happening around him or her.

If the person isn't sure how to answer the questions— he or she may honestly not know if he or she is addicted to cocaine—offer specific examples of things that have happened. Describe what that person does when high, or some of the behavioral and physical signs of concern. The goal is simply to get the person to admit he or she has a problem with cocaine. Such an admission may not be easy, and it may take more than one try.

If a person admits to the problem, offer to help him or her find treatment. Suggest where to go and offer to come along or make any needed appointments. If the person does not admit to a problem, offer to help anyway. It's not unusual for a cocaine addict to deny any problems exist. No one thinks of himself as an out-of-control drug user. Be patient and try again later. Make it clear that help is out there whenever the person wants it. But don't give up.

STEP 5: MAKE CONTACT

A person with a cocaine addiction—either an admitted addict or a user in denial—may not have the strength or motivation to take action. If this is the case, consider doing it for them. Make the initial contact with someone who can help.

Start with a trip to a local drug treatment center or health clinic, or anywhere with resources and people experienced in dealing with drug addicts. Visit it alone or with a trusted adult first to find out what's there. Then arrange to take your friend in need of help. If there's a particular expert to talk to, make an appointment and make the meeting happen.

If there aren't any centers or clinics in the area, make a doctor's appointment for the cocaine-addicted person and offer to go along. It can be hard for an addict to talk to a doctor, especially if the addicted person is not convinced that his or her cocaine use is a real problem. It is helpful to attend the appointment for two reasons: to make sure the addict goes, and to make sure that the problem is described to the doctor honestly and accurately.

If the cocaine addict is in denial, it will likely be difficult to convince him to visit any of these places or meet with anyone about his problem. Although he or she cannot be forced to accept help and treatment, getting help can be strongly encouraged. Simply offering to go along (repeatedly, if necessary) or taking the person to appointments can be a huge push toward getting him to accept help.

If none of this works, get creative. Don't get discouraged. Perhaps having lunch or hanging out with a person who can help is the place to start. The goal is just to make contact. Eventually, the cocaine addict must decide for himself or herself whether or not to seek treatment.

STEP 6: START TREATMENT

Once a cocaine addict admits to a problem and makes contact with someone who can help, he may be ready to begin formal treatment for his addiction. There are a lot of different options for treatment programs, and they can be difficult to navigate alone.

Most cocaine addiction programs include a combination of treatments. Counseling (either individual, group, or family), medication, self-help skills, and behavioral therapy are perhaps the most common pieces of programs for recovering cocaine addicts. Counseling involves simply talking to someone experienced in treating drug addiction. Medications, though not yet perfected, work to ease the brain's chemical dependence on cocaine. Self-help skills teach addicts to cope on their own, without cocaine. And behavioral therapy involves identifying "triggers," meaning certain behaviors, friends, or feelings that prompt cocaine use.

The challenge here is selecting the treatment program that works best for the cocaine addict. In many cases, the cocaine addict will choose whatever program

FACING THE PROBLEM

Tara Palmer-Tomkinson is a British television personality and socialite. She grew up privileged, as a close family friend of the British royal family, and became a well-known party girl in the British press. All of her party-going made getting cocaine especially easy, and her addiction to the drug was life-altering. "I would do more than five grams of coke a day," she said. "In the end, I didn't do lines. . . . I threw the stuff in the air and sniffed clouds of it." After an awkward interview aired on UK television, in which Palmer-Tomkinson appeared disheveled and disoriented, she attended the Meadows Clinic in Arizona to rehabilitate herself.

This June 2005 image of British TV host Tara Parker-Tomkinson shows how years of cocaine abuse made the bridge of her nose collapse. After getting treatment for her addiction, Parker-Tomkinson had plastic surgery to correct the structure of her nose.

(continues on page 104)

(continued from page 103)

In 2006, Tara made headlines in the British press when she admitted that her nasal septum—which separates the nostrils—had collapsed after years of cocaine abuse. The indentation around her nose was obvious, and it was humbling for the often-photographed celebrity.

"You know how you have cartilage inside your nose?" Palmer-Tomkinson told London's *Sunday Mirror*. "Well, I just have fresh air there—a great big space because of all the coke I shoved up it. And it actually hurts if anyone touches it." In 2007, she underwent three hours of surgery to rebuild her nose.

is available and convenient. If there are multiple treatment options in the area, try to choose the best fit.

The National Institute on Drug Abuse (NIDA) breaks cocaine treatment programs into five different categories. Each of NIDA's published treatment manuals tackles cocaine addiction with a slightly different strategy, and only one is targeted to teens. These manuals are described here briefly, and are published on the NIDA Web site at http://www.nida.nih.gov/infofacts/cocaine.html.

If choosing a treatment program seems baffling, this is a place to start. Decide which approach best fits the cocaine addict in need, and then see if there is a similar program in the area.

Manual 1: The Cognitive-Behavioral Approach. The goal of this approach is to teach a drug addict how to get off cocaine. In the words of the manual authors, the user should learn to "recognize the situations in which they are most likely to use cocaine, avoid these situations when appropriate, and cope more effectively with a range of problems and problematic behaviors associated with substance abuse."

Manual 2: The Community Reinforcement Approach. This approach to treating cocaine addiction seeks to strengthen other parts of a cocaine addict's life. This includes family relationships, recreational activities, social networks, and the person's job. The result, it is hoped, is that the addict sees that life is worth living without drugs. The idea is to make life and community so valuable that cocaine becomes less important.

Manual 3: Individual Drug Counseling Approach. Individual drug counseling focuses on the individual. This approach does not involve other family members, friends, or fellow addicts. The focus is on the user's symptoms of drug addiction, related problems, and how to structure recovery for that particular person's needs.

Manual 4: Group Counseling for Cocaine Addiction. Group counseling has four main goals: (1) to inform users on the facts of cocaine addiction, (2) to make addicts more aware of how personal problems are associated with cocaine addiction, (3) to give and receive support for cocaine addiction, and (4) to learn skills to recover from the addiction.

Manual 5: Brief Strategic Family Therapy for Adolescent Drug Abuse. The family therapy approach for teen drug abuse assumes that what affects one family member affects all family members. This treatment method looks at the family as a whole and tries to determine the reasons for an adolescent's cocaine use and related behavior problems.

IT CAN BE DONE

It takes only one use of cocaine to create a new cocaine addict; but it may take a little trial and error to find the right treatment program for that addict. Yet it's worth

THE COCAINE VACCINE

There are currently no widespread, effective medications to treat cocaine addiction. Yet, in 2004, scientists at the British medical company Xenova Pharmaceuticals created and tested a **vaccine** to treat cocaine addiction.

A vaccine works by introducing small amounts of a disease-causing organism into the human body and prompting the body to come up with ways to fight it. Because a vaccine includes such small amounts of the disease, the patient is rarely in danger of catching the disease from the vaccine itself. Once the body's disease fighters are in place, the immune system knows what to do when the actual disease enters the body: It fights the disease and keeps the person from getting sick.

The cocaine vaccine works in a similar way. It introduces small amounts of cocaine to the body—but the cocaine is attached to big molecules of protein. When the body sees this type of protein molecule, it creates cocaine fighters that stop the cocaine from entering the brain. As a result, when the person takes cocaine recreationally, the new cocaine meets these fighters in the body and cannot reach the brain. Because cocaine never reaches the brain,

the time. Finding the best-fit treatment program is important—different treatment programs work better for different people. The right approach can help a person beat a cocaine addiction. It can be done.

the person never gets high on the drug. The cocaine simply doesn't work.

The scientists first tested the vaccine on groups of cocaine users in the United States and results were widely reported by the media. One article, published by the British Broadcasting Corporation (BBC) in June 2004, reported that of those receiving the vaccine, "almost half the addicts were able to stay cocaine-free for six months."

The problem with the cocaine vaccine, however, is that it only treats the cocaine addiction *physically*, not *mentally*. It does not address why the user tried cocaine in the first place. If the user took cocaine to deal with other life problems, he or she is likely to just find another drug to help deal with those same problems. The vaccine cannot combat the mental causes for why a drug user takes a drug.

Although the cocaine vaccine was first tested many years ago, it is still being tested in the United States by the National Institute on Drug Abuse and other government drug agencies.

GLOSSARY

AIDS   A disease that causes the body's immune system (the system that fights off sickness and infection) to stop working

Addiction   A condition of the body and/or brain characterized by needing a substance, such as cocaine, in order to function normally.

Alveoli   Small, root-like tubes with tiny air sacs on the ends, located inside the lungs

Amine   A type of molecule with a specific list of chemical ingredients. Cocaine is a type of amine.

Atom   The smallest piece of an element that still maintains the characteristics of that element

Autonomic nervous system   The parts of the body that work automatically and without thought, such as the heartbeat

Brain   The physical bodily organ contained in the head; refers to all the cells, connections, and chemical processes that happen inside the brain

Cilia   Hair-like cells that line the lungs and clean inhaled air before it enters the bloodstream

Cocaethylene   A new substance formed when the elements contained in cocaine and alcohol molecules rearrange in the liver

Cocaine hydrochloride   The salt form of cocaine

Cocaine psychosis   A disease in which people often see, hear, and feel things in a distorted way

Compulsive behavior   Behavior that a person engages in automatically, without thinking about it

Crack cocaine   A form of cocaine created when powdered cocaine is boiled together with baking soda and water

Craving   An intense, almost irresistible urge to use a drug or other substance

Dendrites   The branch-like tails on the ends of brain cells; used to pass chemicals back and forth

Dopamine   A natural chemical in the brain that controls feelings of pleasure

Element   A substance that cannot be changed into another substance through normal chemical means; the simplest natural substances in the universe

Limbic system   The system in the brain that makes and moves dopamine

Mind   The feelings and actions that result from all the things happening inside the physical brain

Neurotransmitters   Chemicals that move between cells in the brain to pass along communication

Norepinephrine   A chemical in the brain that prepares the body for an emergency; makes the heart beat faster and increases breathing

Nostrils   Two chambers in the nose, separated by the septum

Powdered cocaine   Probably the most well-known form of cocaine

Pure cocaine   Cocaine straight from the coca leaf; packed into crystal-like forms often described as pearly rather than powdered

Precipitate   A solid substance that forms and sinks to the bottom of a liquid when the liquid is boiled

Septum   A wall of cartilage (dense connective tissue) that separates the two chambers of the nostrils

Sinus   The air pockets inside the nose

Stimulant   A drug that does two things: stimulates, or increases, physical activities in the human body (such as the heart beat and breathing); and causes feelings of happiness and other positive emotions for a brief period of time

Vaccine   A small amount of a disease-causing organism that is introduced to the human body, prompting the body to come up with ways to fight the particular disease

Withdrawal   The physical symptoms that a person experiences when an addicted drug is removed from his or her system; may include shaking, chills, nausea, and other extremely uncomfortable physical problems

BIBLIOGRAPHY

Apel, Melanie. *Cocaine and Your Nose: The Incredibly Disgusting Story.* New York: Rosen Publishing Group, 2006.

Associated Press. "Your Brain on Cocaine." January 1, 2003. Available online. URL: http://www.cbsnews.com/stories/2003/01/01/health/main534934.shtml. Accessed January 13, 2007.

Bayer, Linda N., and Steven L. Jaffe, eds. *Junior Drug Awareness: Crack and Cocaine.* New York: Chelsea House, 1999.

BBC. "Cocaine vaccine 'stops addiction.'" June 14, 2004. Available online. URL: http://news.bbc.co.uk/1/hi/health/3804741.stm. Accessed April 29, 2007.

Department of Health and Human Services, Substance Abuse and Mental Health Services Administration, Office of Applied Studies. *2005 National Survey on Drug Use and Health.* Available online. URL: http://www.oas.samhsa.gov/nsduhLatest.htm. Accessed April 4, 2007.

Department of Health and Human Services, Substance Abuse and Mental Health Services Administration, Drug and Alcohol Services Information System. *The DASIS Report.* Available online. URL: http://oas.samhsa.gov/2k5/CocaineTX/CocaineTX.htm. Accessed January 13, 2007.

Department of Justice, Drug Enforcement Administration. "Cocaine." Available online. URL: http://www.usdoj.gov/dea/concern/cocaine.html. Accessed April 22, 2007.

Department of Justice, Drug Enforcement Administration. "Operation Journey." Available online. URL: http://www.usdoj.gov/dea/major/journey.htm. Accessed April 22, 2007.

Greater Dallas Council on Alcohol and Drug Abuse Web site. *www.gdcada.org/statistics/cocaine/stat.htm.* Accessed June 20, 2007.

Gorman, Jessica. "Chemistry Catches Cocaine at Source." Science News Online, November 18, 2000. Available online. URL: http://www.sciencenews.org/articles/20001118/fob1.asp. Accessed April 29, 2007.

Karch, Steven B. *A Brief History of Cocaine*. Boca Raton, Fla.: Taylor and Francis Group, 2006.

Larry King Live. "Interview with Dennis Quaid." CNN.com Transcripts. Aired March 12, 2002. Available online. URL: http://transcripts.cnn.com/TRANSCRIPTS/0203/12/lkl.00. html. Accessed April 29, 2007.

Malone, Carole. "Interview: Tara Palmer-Tomkinson." Sunday Mirror, March 12, 2000. Available online: *http:// findarticles.com/p/articles/mi_qn4161/is_20000312/ ai_n14501443/pg_3*

Mayo Clinic. "Drug Addiction." October 5, 2005. Available online. URL: http://www.mayoclinic.com/health/ drug-addiction/DS00183/DSECTION=2. Accessed April 30, 2007.

Medical News Today. "Strength Of Cocaine Cravings Linked To Brain Response." March 2006. Available online. URL: http://www.medicalnewstoday.com/medicalnews. php?newsid=39593. Accessed April 18, 2007.

MedlinePlus. "Cocaine Withdrawal." U.S. National Library of Medicine and the National Institutes of Health. Available online. URL: http://www.nlm.nih.gov/medlineplus/ency/ article/000947.htm. Accessed April 18, 2007.

Moeller, Rachael. "Cocaine Curtails Body's Ability to Cool Off." *Scientific American*, June 4, 2002. Available online. URL: http://www.sciam.com/article.cfm?articleID= 0009E0C0-D962–1CFC-93F6809EC5880000&sc=I100322. Accessed January 13, 2007.

National Institute on Drug Abuse. "InfoFacts: Crack and Cocaine." Available online. URL: http://www.nida.nih.gov/ infofacts/cocaine.html. Accessed January 15, 2007.

National Institute on Drug Abuse. *Research Report Series: Cocaine Abuse and Addiction*. NIH Publication Number 99–4342. Revised November 2004. Available online. URL: http://www.drugabuse.gov/ResearchReports/Cocaine/ cocaine2.html#what.

Office of National Drug Control Policy. "Drug Facts: Cocaine." Available online. URL: www.whitehousedrugpolicy.gov/drugfact/cocaine/index.html. Accessed January 11, 2007.

Thomson and Gale Publishing. "Richard Pryor." Black History, biographies. Available online. URL: http://www.gale.com/free_resources/bhm/bio/pryor_r.htm. Accessed April 11, 2007.

The United Nations Office on Drugs and Crime. *2006 World Drug Report.* Available online. URL: http://www.unodc.org/pdf/WDR_2006/wdr2006_volume2.pdf. Accessed April 18, 2007.

Walter J. Freeman Neurophysiology Laboratory, University of California at Berkeley. *Effects of Cocaine and Alcohol Consumption.* Available online. URL: http://sulcus.berkeley.edu/mcb/165_001/papers/manuscripts/_314.html. Accessed January 24, 2007.

Whitten, Lori. "Topiramate Shows Promise in Cocaine Addiction." National Institute on Drug Abuse, May 2005. Available online. URL: http://www.nida.nih.gov/NIDA_notes/NNVol19N6/Topiramate.html. Accessed May 9, 2007.

Whitten, Lori. "Disulfiram Reduces Cocaine Abuse." National Institute on Drug Abuse, August 2005. Available online. URL: http://www.nida.nih.gov/NIDA_notes/NNvol20N2/Disulfiram.html. Accessed May 9, 2007.

Xenova. "TA-CD." Available online. URL: http://www.xenova.co.uk/dc_ta_cd.html. Accessed May 1, 2007.

FURTHER READING

Apel, Melanie. *Cocaine and Your Nose: The Incredibly Disgusting Story.* New York: Rosen Publishing Group, 2006.

Augustyn Lawton, Sandra, ed. *Drug Information for Teens: Health Tips About the Physical and Mental Effects of Substance Abuse.* Detroit, Mich.: Omnigraphics, 2006.

Bayer, Linda N., and Steven L. Jaffe, eds. *Junior Drug Awareness: Crack and Cocaine.* New York: Chelsea House, 2000.

Carlson-Berne, Emma. *The History of Drugs: Cocaine.* Chicago: Greenhaven Press, 2005.

Landau, Elaine. *Cocaine.* London: Franklin Watts, 2003.

Lennard-Brown, Sarah. *Cocaine.* Orlando, Fla.: Raintree Publishing, 2004.

Wagner, Heather Lehr. *Drugs: The Straight Facts: Cocaine.* New York: Chelsea House, 2003.

WEB SITES

DRUG ENFORCEMENT ADMINISTRATION: DEMAND REDUCTION
http://www.justthinktwice.com

The U.S. Drug Enforcement Agency's Web site for young people is packed with current drug facts, news, and information in a slick and stylish format.

MONITORING THE FUTURE
http://www.monitoringthefuture.org

The Web site of this ongoing national study examines "the behaviors, attitudes, and values of American secondary school students, college students, and young adults." The site includes survey questions on cocaine use and abuse among these age groups.

THE NATIONAL INSTITUTE ON DRUG ABUSE: COCAINE INFORMATION
http://www.nida.nih.gov/DrugPages/Cocaine.html

Here you can find the most current research reports on cocaine use and abuse in the United States. The site includes basic cocaine facts, statistics, and trends.

THE NATIONAL INSTITUTE ON DRUG ABUSE FOR TEENS: THE SCIENCE BEHIND DRUG ABUSE

http://teens.drugabuse.gov

More drug facts from the NIDA in addition to "Real Stories" and answers to frequently asked questions.

NEUROSCIENCE FOR KIDS: COCAINE

http://faculty.washington.edu/chudler/coca.html

Scientists at the University of Washington present a brief summary of the history and science of cocaine.

OFFICE OF NATIONAL DRUG CONTROL POLICY

http://www.whitehousedrugpolicy.gov

The ONDCP Web site contains reliable information on drugs, drug use, law enforcement, treatment, and prevention.

TEEN DRUG ABUSE

http://www.teendrugabuse.us

This Web site focuses on teen drug use information in the United States. It is not intended to offer treatment or counseling—just information about this nationwide problem—and includes information on cocaine, marijuana, smoking, over-the-counter drugs, and more.

PICTURE CREDITS

INDEX

ABOUT THE AUTHORS

KRISTA WEST has written biology books for young adults on topics as diverse as biofeedback, urinary tract infections, and carbon chemistry. She earned a zoology degree from the University of Washington in Seattle and master's degrees in earth science and journalism from Columbia University. West has been writing about science for newspapers, magazines, and book publishers for more than 10 years. She lives in Fairbanks, Alaska, with her husband and two sons.

Series introduction author **RONALD J. BROGAN** is the Bureau Chief for the New York City office of D.A.R.E. (Drug Abuse Resistance Education) America, where he trains and coordinates more than 100 New York City police officers in program-related activities. He also serves as a D.A.R.E. regional director for Oregon, Connecticut, Massachusetts, Maine, New Hampshire, New York, Rhode Island, and Vermont. In 1997, Brogan retired from the U.S. Drug Enforcement Administration (DEA), where he served as a special agent for 26 years. He holds bachelor's and master's degrees in criminal justice from the City University of New York.